Back in the Beforetime

Back in the Beforetime

TALES OF THE CALIFORNIA INDIANS

Retold by Jane Louise Curry

Illustrated by James Watts

Margaret K. McElderry Books
NEW YORK

Margaret K. McElderry Books
Macmillan Publishing Company
866 Third Avenue
New York, NY 10022
Collier Macmillan Canada, Inc.

Composition by Maryland Linotype Composition Company
Baltimore, Maryland
Printed and bound by R. R. Donnelley & Sons
Harrisonburg, Virginia
Designed by Barbara A. Fitzsimmons

First Edition
Printed in the United States of America
10 9 8 7 6 5 4 3 2 1

Library of Congress Cataloging-in-Publication Data

Curry, Jane Louise.
Back in the beforetime.

Summary: A retelling of twenty-two legends about
the creation of the world from a variety of California
Indian tribes.
1. Indians of North America—California—Legends.
2. Indians of North America—Legends. [1. Indians
of North America—California—Legends] I. Watts,
James, 1955– ill. II. Title.
E78.C15C79   1987   398.2'089970794 [398.2]   86-21339
ISBN 0–689–50410–1

Contents

Back in the Beforetime

How Old Man Above Created the World

Back in the Beforetime, when the World was new as new and flat as flat, Old Man Above, who had made it, sat above the sky and puzzled what to do with it. The World floated far below, wrapped up in the deep dark, for it was so new that the stars were still unlit.

Old Man Above wondered if his World would do to live in. For how was he to tell? His eyes were sharp—sharp enough to spy the Wind—but he could not see down through the dark.

After a while he decided to step down for a closer look, but the dark was too deep and the World too far below. He could not. So he took from the pouch hanging on a cord around his neck a sharp stone knife. With the knife he sliced a neat slit in the sky. Then he gathered up great heaps of ice and snow and swept them down the hole he had made. The ice and snow fell through the clouds, piling up and up beneath the slit in the sky. The pile grew so high that it spilled out across the wide plains, until its peak touched the clouds.

Old Man Above was pleased. He stepped down through the hole onto the closest cloud, then down and down from one dark cloud to the next until he set foot upon the snowy peak.

From his mountaintop, Old Man Above could see the plain below. A little light to see by shone down through the slit in the sky, and so the plain was no longer dark. The light was not bright, or indeed very warm, but the snow that covered the World began to melt, and as it melted, Old Man Above saw that the foothills and flatlands were brown and empty. He stepped down the steep, snowy mountainside and when he reached its foot he found that the ground of the foothills and wide fields was soft.

"Hai! This will be Forest," he said. And with his finger he pushed holes in the earth, here a few and there a lot. In these he planted trees. The melting snow gathered itself into trickles, the trickles into creeks, and the creeks into streams. And the waters watered the trees, and the trees grew. Some grew into oaks and others willows, some pines and some pinyons.

Then Old Man Above took up the leaves that fell and breathed on them, and the leaves became birds and flew away. He cut a stick from the tallest tree, and broke it into three pieces. From the small end he shaped fishes and set them to swimming in the streams that ran down from the ice mountain. Out of the stick's middle Old Man Above made

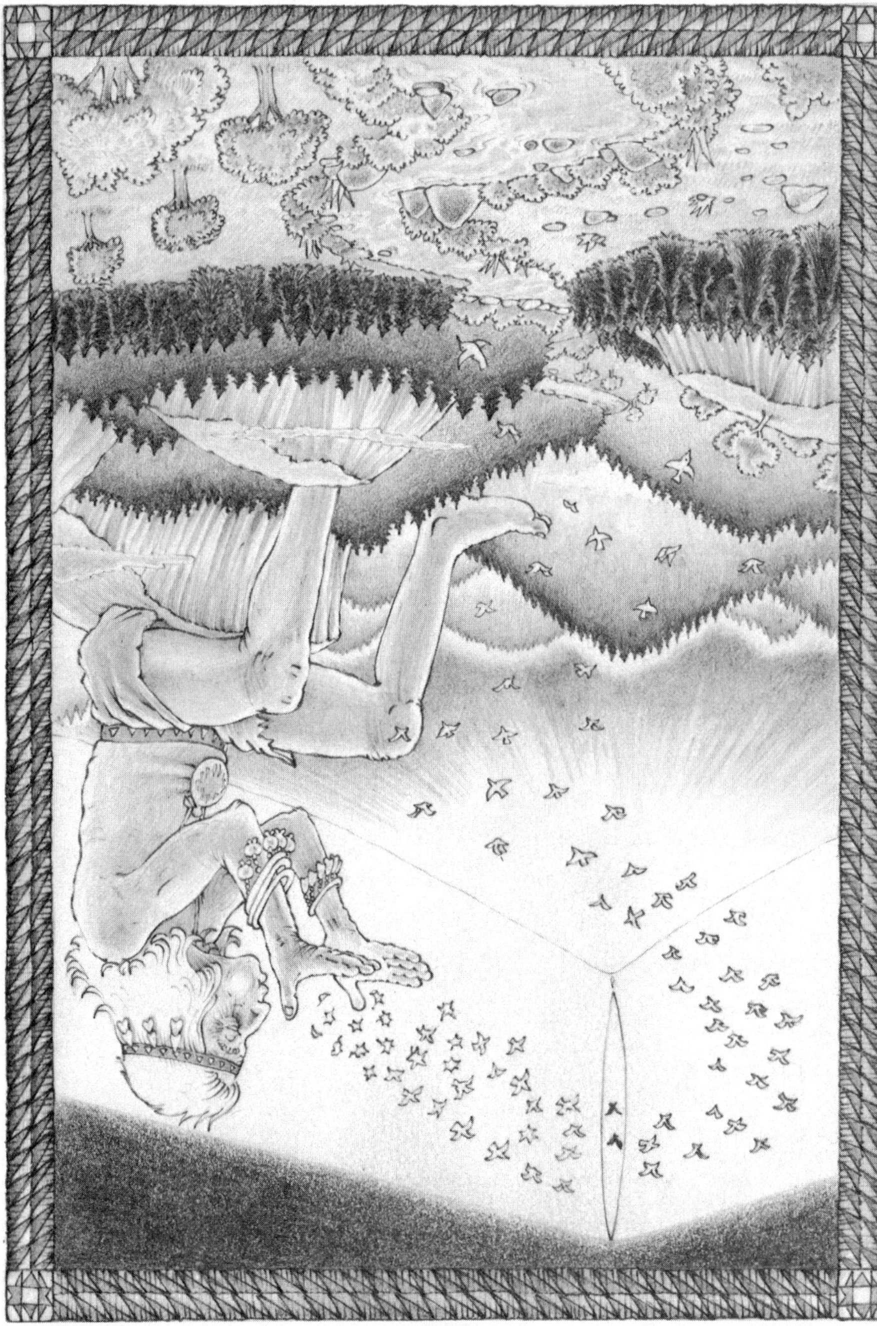

the animal people, all but one. Last of all, from the thick end of the stick he made Grizzly Bear, larger than the others, and stronger and more cunning.

"You, Grizzly," said he, "will walk upon two feet and carry a great club, and be master of all."

But Old Man Above made the great bear too well. Grizzly was so large and so strong that at his growl even Old Man Above trembled.

"Ai! Even I am not safe," he cried, and he wished for a place to hide. So great was his fear that he returned to the steep ice mountain and began to hollow it out for a teepee.

The mountain made a fine home, white and pointed, with fine strong walls, and Old Man Above settled in to watch what happened in the World below. The animal people never saw him again, but now and then they spied the smoke spiraling up from the smokehole of the white teepee mountain and knew he was still there.

They called his mountain Shasta. And so do we, for it still is there.

Roadrunner's Pack

Back in the Beforetime, Weasel and his brother Mink lived in a house not far from the foot of the mountain trail. One fine morning Roadrunner came stepping down that trail. On his back he carried a large sack, and he strode along with his eyes on the road.

Now, Mink had gone out hunting and left young Weasel behind to guard their house. But Little Brother Weasel liked to roam the plain, to sniff out interesting tracks, fresh mouseholes, or whatever was new. And so that Mink would not know he was away from home, when Weasel left he took off his tail and hung it down inside the smokehole.

"Now, Tail," said Little Brother Weasel, "if Mink comes hunting nearby and calls, 'Are you there?' you must answer, 'I am here!'"

Little Brother Weasel had not fared far from the house when he spied Roadrunner hurrying toward him down the track. As Roadrunner passed, Weasel turned and trotted along on his short little legs beside him.

"Hai, there, friend! What can you be carrying in so big a sack as that?"

Roadrunner made no answer. He only stepped along a little faster.

"Come, friend. Let me have a peek in your pack," Little Brother Weasel wheedled.

Roadrunner walked on briskly without a word. Weasel hurried along too, sometimes dashing ahead, sometimes falling behind, sometimes keeping step. And all the while he teased Roadrunner to tell what it was that he carried.

"Hee! Why not sit down awhile to rest?" wheezed Little Brother Weasel. He scurried backward in front of Roadrunner. "That must be a heavy load you carry."

Roadrunner kept right on as if he had not heard.

At last Little Brother Weasel lost his temper. "Tso!" he snarled, and he jumped. He knocked Roadrunner flat and pulled the sack from his back.

"I shall see for myself, old Beak-in-the-Air!" said he, and he bit through the cord that bound it. Dozens of smaller bundles tumbled out of the sack to roll upon the ground.

"Hai, hee!" cried Little Brother Weasel. He rubbed his paws together in glee and snatched up one of the little bundles.

Roadrunner picked himself up in a daze and shook the dust from his feathers. When he saw what Weasel meant to do, he opened his beak to shrill a warning. But he was too late.

As Little Brother Weasel pulled open the little bundle, a great cloud of darkness spilled out. It filled the sky and poured across the plain. Soon all the World was dark. "Hee, hai!" cried Weasel, groping on the ground. He could not see his paw in front of his nose, but in his excitement he cared nothing for that. He found another of the little bundles and snatched that up too and tore it open. A cloud of stars flew out.

The pack held bundles of many sizes and shapes, and Weasel pulled open every one he could put a paw to. The Moon and each of the big stars—Morning Star, Evening Star, Pole Star—were wrapped up in a separate bundle. Rain was tied up in one, snow in another. All the weathers there were in the world were in Roadrunner's pack. Clouds, sleet, whirlwinds, breezes, fogs, and freezes: everything was there, and Little Brother Weasel, squealing "Ho, hai, hee!" set them loose upon the earth.

But when the weathers had whirled away, Weasel found himself alone in the dark, and lost. Roadrunner did not answer his call. The winds and rains had washed away the trail. Little Brother Weasel ran here and there, back and forth, this way and that, but could not find his way home.

"Hai, Brother Mink!" he cried, frightened at last. "Help me!"

. . .

Now Mink, Weasel's brother, was hunting near home when the darkness fell.

"Little Brother Weasel, are you there?" called he in a loud voice.

"I am here," piped up Little Brother Weasel's tail, hanging in the smokehole.

Mink went a little way, then called again.

"Are you there, my brother?"

"I am here," called Little Brother Weasel's tail.

In this fashion, calling and listening, Mink made his way home. There, he discovered the trick his brother had played with his tail. "Hai, here is Little Brother Weasel's tail, but where can the rest of him be?" Mink wondered. And he looked in the storage baskets and under the sleeping mats.

Then, faint as a whisper, he heard Little Brother Weasel himself wailing "Brother Mink!" from far off through the darkness.

"Tso! Little Brother Weasel has been up to mischief again!" Mink thought. So he made no answer.

Weasel called again, and yet again, but still Mink made no answer.

Mink let Little Brother Weasel wander for a long while in the darkness, back and forth and up and down and roundabout, calling out, "Brother Mink! Where are you?" Then, when he judged that Weasel had learned his lesson, Mink took out his obsidian knife and threw it upward, hard, against the darkness. The knife cut a hole that let down a little of the light that shone through the slit in the sky above the mountain.

And so Weasel found his way home at last.

But had he not let loose the bundle of darkness, our nights would not be so long and dark in the wintertime.

3

How Coyote Stole the Sun

Back in the Beforetime, while the darkness Little Brother Weasel let loose still lay deep on the plain, every day was worse than the last. The animal people went around in circles. They bumped into each other and trees and their own houses. The bird people flew up and down, crashing into each other or the treetops or the ground. The darkness was so thick on the plain that it swallowed up even the light of the stars Little Brother Weasel had spilled from Roadrunner's bundle. And the darkness was full of the fog he had freed.

It was terrible. Fur and feathers grew damp. The ground grew cold. Teeth chattered. Beaks clattered. No one knew when to get up or go to sleep. The trees lost their leaves, and the grass withered. At first there was plenty to eat, for the oak trees dropped all their acorns, but only Wolf and Fox and Coyote, who had keen noses, had any luck at hunting. Even so, it was not long before they too grew lean and bony with hunger, for as they blundered about in the dark the deer could hear them coming, and the rabbits and mice kept to their holes.

"Tell us what to do," said the animal people of the plain to Sandhill Crane, their medicine man. "Tell us what to do," begged the animals who found their way to his house. "Tell us what to do," pleaded the folk who bumped into him in the dark. Crane could only sigh, for he had no answer.

Ki-yoo the Coyote grew angry. "If Crane does not know what to do," Coyote thought, "he should make something up. Something is better than nothing."

And because something is better than nothing, Coyote ate up his last acorn, and trotted out into the darkness. There *must* be a better place for animal folk to live. And he, Coyote, would find it! He followed his nose to the river, the river to a creek, and the creek to a trickle of water that slid down from the foothills of the white-teepee mountain.

There, at the hill's foot, his nose caught a shimmer of a whiff of a sniff of the most delicious aroma he had ever smelled. It was nothing like the clear fresh tang of trout. It did not have the sharp, rich aroma of freshly killed venison. Yet even so, it brought to his mind mouthwatering visions of bounding deer and leaping fish.

So Coyote followed his nose.

As he trotted up into the Foothills Country he could think of nothing but the scent he followed.

He did not notice the dim light ahead until after a while the darkness around him gave way to gloom. Bare, shadowy trees appeared along the trail, and suddenly Coyote saw that he could see.

"Ha, hai! What can this mean?" thought he, and he trotted on all the faster.

Ahead, the light was brighter still. The trees wore leaves. The country began to be dry and warm. And the delicious smell was stronger than ever. When at last Coyote came near the place where the light was brightest, he spied the village of the Foothills People ahead.

Now, hungry Coyote might be, and brave, but he was cautious and cunning too. He sat and waited and watched. He waited until a fox, one of the Foothills People, left the village and came trotting down the path with his bow and quiver of arrows slung over his back.

"Hai, now we shall see!" thought Coyote.

In the twitch of a whisker he changed himself into a fox just like the other. The shadings on his fur, the notch in one ear torn in an old fight—all was the same. As Coyote-Fox trotted up the trail Fox had trotted down, he grinned. Not even Fox's mother could have told the difference between them, for Coyote's magic was strong. But, magic or no, the closer he came to the Foothills Village, the lower Coyote's bushy tail drooped and the harder he panted in the heat of the light in the sky above.

For the village had a Sun!

A Sun that hung from the sky on a rope.

In the village not a head turned as Coyote passed among the lodges. When he stopped to drink from a pitch-lined water basket, the pups and kits nearby did not pause in their play. One of the wives looked up from stirring soup in a cooking basket by the fire where cooking stones heated and acorn cakes baked. But she turned back to her work, and Coyote-Fox trotted on to the next fire circle.

Cookfires! Coyote marveled. The Foothills People had not only a Sun, but cookfires! The wonderful aroma that had drawn him through the darkness must have come from the haunch of venison roasting on the spit of the second fire. Its fat sizzled and spat and dripped onto the red coals. It smelled not at all like raw venison. Coyote sniffed, and shivered with pleasure. He touched the meat and quickly licked the juice from his paw. Hai, hee! It tasted as good as it smelled. His empty stomach rumbled as he turned away.

"I have seen what I came to see," Coyote told himself. "I must go before Fox returns."

But then his stomach growled again, as loudly as any grizzly. And he could not bear to go. So he did not. He stayed, sleeping in the shade, until the chief of the animal wives called everyone to eat. Coyote-Fox ate his fill of mush and fish and roasted meat, and afterward slipped away. Changing back into his own shape, he turned his nose toward the downhill path and hurried toward the dark below.

Down in the dark, Coyote returned by the way he had come. He followed his nose to the trickle of water, and followed the trickle to the creek to the river. But between the riverbank and the village on the plain he lost his way more than once. When at last he reached home he hurried to tell Crane of the wonderful land where the animal folk had not only a Sun and fire and good food, but wives and pups and kits and chicks.

"It is truly wonderful," exclaimed Coyote.

Crane was not so sure, for he was fearful of all things new. "The dark is bad, but this Sun sounds dangerous. It could burn our eyes and feathers and fur."

Coyote was alarmed. "Must we sit in the dark and starve, then? The hunters of the Foothills People have light to see and shoot by, and the wives bake acorn cakes and roast good meat. But we have no food to feed wives, and with no wives we have no pups or chicks."

Crane tossed his beak in pride. "We are strong. We have no need of what we do not have. If *you* must have them, then go back to your Foothills People."

Coyote went off and away in a huff.

"And so I will!" said he.

Once back in the foothills Coyote waited in the bushes by the village trail until he spied a bobcat coming out to hunt. Once the bobcat was past, he turned himself into just such a one. Bobcat's wife could not have told the difference. Brown-spotted coat, tufted ears—every hair was the same.

In the village Coyote-Bobcat made himself at home again. He ate the good food. He watched the pups at play. He admired the Sun. It was wonderful even though it was very hot. And yet . . .

And yet, Coyote could not be happy. He could not forget his people in the flatlands. How could he be happy while they hungered and shivered down in the dismal dark?

There was nothing to do but go home again.

As soon as he reached his own village, Coyote sniffed Crane out and told him again how pleasant life in the Foothills Village was.

"And they take the Sun down at night so they can sleep. In the morning, if a cookfire has gone out, they poke a stick in the Sun to get fire to light it again. Then they hang the Sun up and have light to hunt and gather acorns by. A Sun is a wonderful thing. If we had one, you would like it. I know you would."

Crane rattled his feathers and hunched over against the cold. "Perhaps," said he, but still he was not sure.

"We could try to buy it," Coyote said eagerly.

"Not so fast, Ki-yoo!" Crane shifted from one long leg to the other. "I know you! You would bring this Sun here with no thought how we could make it work. How would we hang it up? Our plain is much farther from the sky than the foothills are."

"I will think of something," Coyote said, and he pestered Crane until at last, to be rid of him, Crane agreed that Coyote should ask the Foothills People how much shell money they would take for the Sun.

And so it was that Coyote went in his own skin to the Foothills Village to learn how much the Sun would cost. But the animal people there would name no price. Sell their Sun? Never! Not even a sliver of it. And they ran at Coyote and bit at his heels and chased him down into the foggy dark.

After the Foothills People turned back to their village, Coyote sat on a log on the border between the dusk and the dark, and thought. They would not sell the Sun. So he would have to steal it. That

would not be easy. The Sun was kept at night in a
house made of sod with no window at all. Its door
was guarded by Turtle, Sun's Keeper, and Turtle
guarded it well. He slept for no more than two or
three minutes at a time, and when he slept he kept
one eye open wide. It was said by the Foothills
People that at the fall of a leaf on the roof near the
smokehole, or the pit-pat of the smallest foot past
the door, the Keeper of the Sun would be up, with
an arrow ready to his bow.

How, Coyote puzzled, could he steal the Sun
without stealing Turtle too?

At last he thought of a plan. He crept back up
the trail and hid himself in a clump of bushes below
the village. When the hunters came out again in the
late afternoon to hunt, Turtle came too, gathering
twigs and broken branches for firewood.

Quickly Coyote circled up and around. When he
saw Turtle returning, he lay down across the top of
the trail and turned himself into a large, crooked
oak tree limb.

"Hai!" cried Turtle. "What luck! This will burn
slowly and last all night." He set aside the pine
boughs he had gathered and hoisted the heavy limb
onto his back to carry it to Sun's house. There he
dropped it atop the woodpile beside the fire circle
and went to gather more before dinner. Coyote-

Limb lay still. He was glad indeed that a tree limb could not feel hunger, for the smell of good meat roasting filled the house.

After the evening meal, the Sun was brought in for the night and put in a basket across the fire from Coyote-Limb. Turtle built up the fire, then picked up the limb and placed one end in the fire. But it would not stay. Because it was crooked, it would not lie flat.

"Limb, lie flat on the fire and burn!" scolded Turtle, but every time he pushed it down, up it turned again. At last he lost his temper, lifted it up, and dropped it—plop!—in a shower of sparks across the fire. One end fell close to the basket in which the Sun slept.

"Burn from the middle out, then!" snapped Turtle. Turning away, he did not see that, because of Coyote's magic, the limb did not burn at all.

Coyote watched and waited until Turtle settled down with one eye on the door. "Sleep, Turtle," he sang under his breath. "*Upija, upija.* Sleep, sleep."

Turtle's head drooped little by little until at last his chin rested on the floor. One eye closed and then, very slowly, the other. Soon Turtle began to snore.

Coyote-Limb tilted silently toward the Sun. Then, changing quickly back to his own shape, he hopped off the fire, popped a lid over the Sun,

snatched up the basket, and dashed out and away.

Turtle awoke at once. "Hai!" he shouted out. "The Sun is gone! Someone has stolen the Sun!"

All of the Foothills People ran out into the night, crying, "Thief! Thief!" But they could not discover which way Coyote had gone, for he, coming from the land where all was night, was more sure-footed in the dark than they. While they bumped into each other and cried, "Thief! Thief!" Coyote bounded down through the foothills and into the darker dark below. When the cries of "Thief!" had died away behind him, Coyote lifted the basket lid enough to light his way, and trotted straight home, smiling to think what a welcome he would have.

But it was not the welcome he looked for. When the animal people of Coyote's village saw the Sun they covered their eyes and ran into their houses. They shouted and scolded and would not come out until Coyote covered it up again.

"It hurts our eyes!"

"Hai, how bright!"

"How are we to sleep with that shining through the thatch?"

"Take it away!"

Coyote took the basket to Crane, but Crane was afraid too, and would not take it.

"It was your idea," said Crane to Coyote. "*I*

don't know what to do with it. We cannot hang it from the sky as your Foothills People do. If you wish to keep this Sun, Ki-yoo, you must think what to do with it."

Coyote went off in a huff. His friends were freezing in the damp and dark, and not a one of them had thanked him. Hai, ha! He would show them!

So Coyote slung Sun's basket on his back and traveled west to the place where the sky's edge meets the earth's edge. There, at the West Hole in the Sky, he took Sun out of his basket and ordered him to roll out through the hole and down under the World until he came to the East Hole in the Sky. When he arrived there, he was to come up and travel west, shining first on the Foothills People, and then on the plain. When he came again to the West Hole, he was to go under the world as before so the animal people could sleep. And every day he must do the same.

Because Coyote's magic was strong, Sun obeyed.

And when morning came and Sun rolled up across the sky, Crane and the others were glad at last. They could see where they were going. The days were warm. There was game to hunt. And all the trees and grasses grew again.

4

Mountain-Making

Back in the Beforetime, in the days after the Sun was put in the sky, the animal people could see at last how wide and empty the World was. The plains stretched north, south, east, and west to the sky's edge. In all the World there were no landmarks but the white-teepee mountain Shasta and the lake that was called Tulare. On the lake lived all the swimmers and divers among the Beforetime People. The ducks lived there, and the geese. Pelican lived there, and Mud Hen. Coyote and Cuckoo, Prairie Fox and Jackrabbit, Jay and Jumping Mouse, and all the others of the bird and animal people lived together in the villages of the foothills or the plain.

Coyote was still full of his own cleverness. Had not his Sun been a great success? Even Crane said so. But before long, the animal people took to turning away when they spied him coming. "Trouble-maker," they called him. "Old Nosy." And "Sneak," because of his silent step as he sidled close to listen to the plans and secrets of others. For Coyote snooped and gossiped and meddled. And always he knew better than anyone else.

"*That* is no way to shell an acorn!" he said.

"*That* is no way to feather an arrow!"

"*That* roof will never keep out rain."

Far worse was his gossip. If Fox told his wife that Skunk's house was not very tidy, Coyote, overhearing, ran at once to tell everyone else. And with each telling, Skunk's house grew untidier.

"Have you heard how Skunk keeps house? His floor is littered with mouse bones."

"Have you heard? Skunk's store baskets hold more maggots than food!"

"Have you not heard? Old Skunk grows worse and worse. His blankets are so stiff with dirt that in the daytime he cannot fold them. He props them up against the wall!"

Afterward, happy as a swallow in spring, Coyote trotted off to tell Skunk that Fox had been telling tales about him.

But then Coyote turned his tongue's mischief on Eagle, chief of all the bird and animal people. Coyote whispered this, and whispered that. He stirred up trouble happily.

"Did you hear what Eagle said about Crane?"

"Is it true that Eagle ate Cottontail's cousin?"

"I hear old Eagle is blind in one eye, and others must do his hunting."

At last Eagle could stand it no more.

"No more!" Eagle shrilled. "I must find somewhere to live where Coyote cannot spread his nonsense."

But where? Coyote wandered everywhere but under the waters of Tulare Lake or on the high mountain slopes.

A mountain! Now there was an idea, thought Eagle.

At once he called the animal people together—all of them but Coyote—to make his announcement. "I am moving away," said Eagle. "Away from the mischief Coyote makes with his meddling and tale-telling. And you shall help me. All of you."

"Tell us what to do," said Bear.

"And where you will live," added Jackrabbit.

Eagle nodded. "Coyote travels the foothills and plains. I must live in the mountains, where he will not go. So you must build me mountains. High mountains, away to the east, where I can make the highest mountaintop home."

Eagle was a good chief, so the bird and animal people did as he asked. With digging sticks they dug earth to fill their burden baskets, and when their baskets were full they slung them on their backs and set out toward the east. At the place where the mountains were to be, they emptied the baskets and returned for more. Beaver went, and

Bear. Fox and Weasel, Cottontail and Caribou worked side by side. Mouse and Mountain Lion and Deer came, and Crow and Pelican, Quail and Rail and Owl, Badger, Otter, and Skunk. Hundreds came. Even Hummingbird, and Ant and all of his people.

As the earth was heaped higher and higher, the mountains rose. Bit by bit they grew until at last they were so tall that the snow began to fall on their crests.

"Enough!" called Eagle. "Enough!"

The bird and animal people stopped at the mountain foot and emptied there on the ground the baskets of earth left over. When they looked up at the mountains they had mounded up, they raised a cheer. Such ridges and ranges! Such fine pointed peaks!

And the round mounds you still may see along the foothills of the Sierras? They are the earth from the baskets left over from building Eagle's new home.

5

Measuring Worm's Great Climb

Back in the Beforetime, for a long while after Coyote put the Sun up in the sky, the animal people had no fire. Coyote, in his haste and bad temper, had forgotten to light a fire from Sun's blaze before he set him up in the sky. So for all his fine promises, the people still had no cookfires to roast their meat. And winter's cold was on its way.

"Where are the flames that flicker like gold, Coyote?" they taunted. "And our tasty crusted roasts?"

Others said bitterly, "What of the coals that chase away the chill of the night? Where are they?"

"And what of the torchfires that lighten the dark?"

At last Coyote could bear no more, and slunk away. "He will be back—worse luck," said some when days had passed, and no Coyote. "He has gone to join the Foothills People," said others, hoping it might be so.

But then one moonlit night Eagle and his son Falcon spied a new wink of light in the sky above their mountain home, and Coyote was forgotten.

"See how it glows and glitters!" said Falcon.

"Could it be fire?"

"It must be fire," Eagle answered. "What else would shine so? It cannot be a star, for the sky is full of clouds." And he stretched his neck out and called.

"*Keeee, keeee!* Come, come! All good climbers come up to me."

And though it was a cold night for climbing, the animals heard his call, and came. Black Lizard came, and Ground Squirrel and Gray Squirrel, Measuring Worm, Ant, and Wildcat. When they reached the ledge below Eagle's perch and asked why he had called them, Eagle pointed out the pin-prick of light above.

"See there—by that flat place in the sky? Tso! There is the fire you have been longing for. I am sure of it. Who among you will climb up to fetch it down?"

The climbers looked at each other, alarmed. What, climb up the sky? So high? Oh, no!

But then they remembered their longing for roasted meat and warm houses, and that longing was stronger than fear.

"Leave it to me," said Wildcat, and he leaped bravely on up the mountain, heading for the sky.

"No, *I* will go!" cried Black Lizard, and he skittered off behind.

"And I!" echoed Ground Squirrel and Gray

Squirrel together as they bounded away.

"I shall go too," piped Ant, and he marched off after them.

"And I," called Measuring Worm, humping slowly behind.

Wildcat was a strong climber, so it was not long before he reached the clouds that sat on the mountaintop. Far overhead, the fire shimmered and winked.

Wildcat climbed onto the nearest cloud and scrambled up into the sky. "What a hero I shall be," thought he, and he bounded higher and higher. At last, the fire-light gleamed just overhead.

But near as it was, it was too far for Wildcat. The sky at that place was high and steep as a cliff. Beneath the flat place a rim thrust sharply outward. Wildcat reached out a paw and dug in his claws. Two—three—four—steps up, and he was under the ledge. He hung almost upside-down. But try as he might, he dared not reach one more inch toward the edge, for fear he would fall. Under his weight his claws were tearing the sky, and the rocks far below were sharp.

Ground Squirrel tried next. He reached the underside of the sky-ledge in no time. But though he was not so heavy as Wildcat, neither were his toenails as strong as claws. He could not climb over the edge.

Gray Squirrel was next to try, but he had no better luck. Ant and Black Lizard fared the same, for though the sky was not hard, it was very smooth. Other climbers came, and some could not even reach the sky. None could climb over the ledge to fetch the light that Eagle said was fire.

At the very last came Measuring Worm.

"Hai, hee!" Measuring Worm laughed to himself. "It is no wonder no one can reach the flat place in the sky. All are afraid they will fall. But not I. I shall take my piece of string!"

Measuring Worm was slow, but he was surefooted. One end of his string he tied around his middle. Then, gripping tightly with his hind feet, he climbed with his front feet until he was stretched up full length. With the very first of his front feet he tied the free end of his string fast. Only then did he walk his hind feet up. Once he had a tight foothold he untied the string and and reached up again with his front feet. Slowly, hump, hump, hump, up he moved. And each time he fastened and unfastened his string, at first to the mountain, then to the clouds, and at last to the sky.

Twice, near the top, Measuring Worm's feet slid on the slippery sky and he fell. Back and forth he swung, high above the earth, dangling from his string. And each time the Wind rose and blew him back against the sky, where he caught on with all his feet and went on climbing. *Hump, hump, hump.*

When he reached the place where the ledge thrust out over his head, Measuring Worm did not stop. Upside-down, he crept out, out to the edge. There he held on with his hind feet and, stretching out, reached over the top with his front feet and tied his string tight to the sky.

Then he took a deep breath and, holding on fiercely with all his front feet, brought his hind feet over the top. Then he raised his head to look for the golden flames.

But there were none.

There was only a small, shiny rock.

"Tso!" said Measuring Worm to himself as he picked up the rock and found it warm and smooth to touch. "So this is what fire looks like! It is nothing like the Sun." He tucked it in his carrying sack and hurried slowly back down the sky.

When he reached the World below, all of the birds and beasts were waiting in the foothills beyond the mountains. Even Coyote was there. "Let us see, let us see!" they cried.

Measuring Worm opened his sack. Falcon plucked out the shiny rock in his beak.

Coyote had crept to the front of the crowd. "*That* is not fire," he scoffed.

All those who had seen the Sun before it was set in the sky agreed. "*That* is not fire," they jeered.

Coyote grinned. "It is Eagle-fire. Old and dim!"

Black Bear shook his great head. "No! There is fire *in* it, just as Eagle has said. Let me have it. I will get the fire out."

Black Bear squeezed the rock. He bit it. He stamped on it. Nothing happened.

Mountain Lion stepped forward. "Let me help," said he. And together he and Black Bear picked up a great boulder and dropped it on the shiny rock, breaking it in two.

And when the two halves were struck together, fire leaped out in little sparks and caught in a clump of dry grass.

The animal people fed the fire, and lit branches to carry it home. But the flames of the fires they lit were pale and warm like the stone, not hot and bright like Sun's. They could take the chill from a house, but not warm it. They could warm food, but not cook it. They could lighten the darkness, but not chase it away.

When Coyote scowled, and looked as if he would complain, Eagle spoke up quickly.

"It is a great pity Coyote did not remember to give us some of the Sun's fire before he set it in the sky. But as Coyote himself so often has told us, something is better than nothing."

And so it was.

6

The Theft of Fire

Back in the Beforetime the animal people liked to gamble. Indeed, they loved to. They would bet on which side up a stone would fall. On how many acorns a basket held. On who would shoot the first squirrel of the day's hunt.

One winter day the Pish-pish, the Yellow Jacket people, came downriver from the World's End to visit Eagle's people. The Pish-pish, as it happened, were greater gamblers still. After the evening meal they sat by the fire circle and played at Toss-stones and the Hand Game with the animal people. First the Yellow Jackets won all of the shell money in the village, then all of the beads. They won all of the acorns and all of the sugar-pine seeds, all of the camas and yampah roots, and all of the baskets these were stored in. They won rabbit-fur robes. They won bird-feather capes and beautiful basket hats. Tobacco, dried fish—they gambled all night and won it all.

When all had been lost, still the Yellow Jacket people said, "We bet all that we have won that the stones will land black side up."

"How can we bet?" asked Eagle. "You have won all that we own."

"Hai, I am sure the stones will fall white side up," cried Coyote. "Let us bet our fire stones."

The Pish-pish laughed. "We have no need of shiny-warm fire stones and shiny-warm fire. At the World's End we have *real* fire, red and hot and dancing."

"And we cannot bet our fire stones," said Eagle to Coyote. "We need them."

"Not if we take care to keep our cookfires burning," Coyote urged. "Come, let us bet!"

And so they did, and again they lost.

Then the Pish-pish put on their new robes over their bright yellow jackets, and packed up their new shell money and beads and seeds in their new baskets and sacks, took up their shiny new fire stones, and set off upriver for their home at the World's End.

No sooner were they out of sight with the magic stones than Skunk's cookfire sputtered and spat and died. Then the fire in Fox's house died. And Duck's. And Mole's. Then Falcon's. And Bobcat's and Coyote's. Even Eagle's. Every fire that had been lit by the fire stones sputtered and spat and died into darkness.

The animal people cried out in alarm and ran to find Eagle. "What shall we do?" they cried.

"Perhaps we can find another fire stone," Eagle said.

The people looked everywhere, but none of the shiny stones they found made fire, and they grew angry and shouted at Coyote.

"This is your doing, Coyote. It was you who said the stones would fall white side up and win back our goods. It was you who bet our fire stones."

"And it is I who will bring them back," Coyote answered, for he liked nothing better than an adventure. "Indeed, I will do more, for the Pish-pish have hotter fire than ours. I will steal some of theirs."

"Foolish Coyote! They can fly faster than you can run," said some.

"That I know," said Coyote. "But I have a plan. Mountain Lion, will you help?"

"I will," said Mountain Lion.

"You, Eagle and Falcon and grandson Chicken Hawk, can fly swift and straight. Will you help?"

"We will," said Eagle and Falcon and Coyote's grandson Chicken Hawk.

"Bear, you are good at running downhill."

"I will come," growled Bear.

Grouse spoke up bravely. "I am good at running downhill under bushes."

Hummingbird asked to go too. "For I can fly too fast to be seen."

"And I—I will go," said Tortoise. "I am not a good runner, but I can pull in my head and legs and roll downhill like a log."

Frog, not to be outdone, said that he would go too. "For I can hop, and I can swim."

"We will come too," said Measuring Worm and Buzzard.

So Coyote tucked a piece of oak bark in his belt and together they went off for the Yellow Jackets' village.

Once across the river, Coyote told Frog to sit down on the riverbank. "Watch for Tortoise," said he. "When he gives you the fire, you must leap into the river and swim for home."

"I will," said Frog.

At the top of the mountain beyond the river, Coyote told Tortoise to sit on the highest place. "Watch for Measuring Worm," said he. "When he gives you the fire, you must roll down to the river and give it to Frog."

"I will," said Tortoise.

At the top of the next mountain ridge, Coyote told Measuring Worm to wait and watch for Bear. "When he gives you the fire," said Coyote, "you must hurry back as fast as you can, and give it to Tortoise."

"I will," said Measuring Worm.

In this way Coyote left his companions behind, one by one, until only Eagle was left. As they drew near the World's End, Eagle's sharp eyes saw smoke away to the north along the mountainside, and away to the south.

"Look! Fires in the forest!" cried Eagle. "The Yellow Jackets are hunting the deer, driving them downhill with fire. See how bright the flames are!"

Coyote's eyes shone, and he grinned. "Wait for me here," said he. "I will go ahead and find the house where they keep this red and gold fire."

When he came to the house at the World's End, Coyote peered in at the smokehole. To his surprise, the fire in its pit was guarded only by the Yellow Jacket children. So he went to the door like any friendly visitor.

"Tso, little ones! Have they left you here all alone?"

"Our parents are out on the mountain hunting," said the little Yellow Jackets. "Who are you?"

"Only a traveler," said Coyote, and he sat himself down by the door. "I will wait till they come."

The little Yellow Jackets came close. They looked at his ears and his nose and his tail.

"The hair on your ears is reddish," said one.

"Your nose is pointed," said another.

"The tip of your tail is dark," said a third.

"We think you are Coyote," said the largest and

bravest of the little Yellow Jackets. "Our parents told us no one but Coyote would dare to come to the World's End."

"Coyote? Me?" Coyote laughed as if that were the greatest of jokes. "I am only his cousin, Dog. I have come to visit the chief of the Pish-pish."

The Yellow Jacket children half believed him. They went back to sit around the bright, beautiful fire. Coyote followed, and smiled and said, "Such handsome children! It would please me to make you more handsome still. Shall I paint your faces for the deer-meat feast you will have tonight?"

To be painted, like full-grown animal warriors! How could they say no? "Yes!" cried the young Yellow Jackets, forgetting their parents' warnings.

So Coyote put his piece of slow-burning bark in the fire until the end was charred, and one by one painted each little face with it and drew handsome black stripes on their bright yellow jackets. When he finished, he put the end of the bark back in the fire, and poured out water into a bowl.

"Come, see yourselves in the water," said Coyote. The little Yellow Jackets crowded around. As they bent over the water to look at their reflections, Coyote picked up the glowing bark with a hind foot so that no one would spy him. "I shall step out to see if your hunters are coming," said he.

Once outside the door, Coyote tucked the oak

bark in his armpit and ran. He ran hard and long, down from the mountain at the World's End, across the valley and up again. At last he reached the place on the next mountain ridge where Eagle waited.

"Hai!" he gasped. "Take the fire and fly. I hear the little Yellow Jackets calling for help."

Eagle took the bright bark in his talons and flew swift as the wind over mountain and hill to the place where Falcon waited.

"Hai! Take the fire and fly!" he cried. "I hear the Yellow Jacket hunters answering their children!"

Falcon flew on, the bark in his beak, until he came to Chicken Hawk's post. "Hai, hurry!" he cried as Chicken Hawk rose into the air. "I can hear the Yellow Jackets singing their war song as they fly."

And so the fire was passed from talon to paw to beak to claw, from Chicken Hawk to Mountain Lion to Buzzard to Grouse to Bear. The Yellow Jackets came buzzing close behind. But each time as they nearly caught the runner, the fire changed hands and the new runner was off and away.

The Yellow Jackets had flown all the way from the World's End, and as the chase went on their wings beat more and more slowly. Even so, they almost caught Bear. Bear ran downhill very fast, but he slowed as he climbed to the next mountain ridge. Measuring Worm waited at the top, and as the Yellow Jackets buzzed up the slope, Measuring Worm balanced the bark on his back and with his magical power humped himself up, and stretched across to the next ridge.

There it was Tortoise's turn. Tortoise took the fire-bark, pulled in his head and legs, and rolled downhill like a bounding, rolling boulder. Faster and faster he went, and at the bottom he bounced toward the riverbank.

The Yellow Jackets were close behind, but Frog sat waiting with his wide mouth open. He caught the fire, and with one hop, hid in the river.

When the Yellow Jackets buzzed up, they looked everywhere, but Frog and the fire were gone. They buzzed back and forth along the riverbank. But they found not even a wisp of smoke, and at last flew away upriver toward the World's End and home.

Frog watched from under the water until the Pish-pish were gone, and climbed out on the far bank. His mouth was so hot that he spat the fire out into a clump of willow trees, and dove in the water for a drink.

When Coyote and the others came straggling back, there was no sign of fire to be seen, no smoke or flame or glowing coal.

"Hai!" cried Coyote. "Where is our fire? Where is Frog?"

"Frog spat it out into the willows, and now it is gone," said Tortoise in sorrow.

"Hai, yi!" wailed Coyote. "How could he do such a loon-witted thing. No wonder he is hiding. Oh, what I would not give to get my paws on him! What shall we do for fire now?"

Frog's head rose above the water. "It is simple," said he, and he hopped out onto the willow bank. There he cut two sticks of willow, and showed the animal people how to cut a small hole in the side of one and twirl the other, like a drill, in the hole. First the dry moss tinder glowed, then a wisp of smoke rose up and grew to a tendril. A little flame licked at the thin twigs of kindling.

And so it is to this day that Yellow Jackets have stripes—and Men can make fire with willow sticks.

7

Coyote and the Salmon

One day back in the Beforetime, Bear and Eagle came home from their fishing with bad news.

"The salmon are gone from the river!" roared Bear.

"We did not see a one," shrieked Eagle in anger.

It was terrible news. Of all the fishes in the river or sea, the salmon was the tastiest. In two days the animal people were to have a feast—and what was a feast without salmon?

"How *can* there be no salmon?" cried Crane.

"Someone has stolen them all," Eagle said sadly.

Gloom settled down on the village like a great, gray cloud. The sun still shone, the grass was still green, and the hunters came home with good meat, but the animal people sighed as they ate, and thought of the feast to come.

No salmon!

Coyote sighed loudest of all, for he loved salmon more than anything in the world. But Coyote was as clever as he was greedy, and so he began to think.

"Who could steal so many fish?" thought he.

"Not Pelican. Where would he hide them? Not Sea Lion. Not even he could eat so many."

Coyote frowned and paced up and down. "It cannot be Fox," said he to himself. Fox's den was near a pond, but his pond could not hold even *thirty* salmon. Thirty thousand had vanished. Or more. Then, too, the animals' path to the north passed along Fox's pond's rim. If there were salmon in it, someone would have seen.

But there were other ponds. One lay below the waterfall near the house of the Ixkareya.

And the two Ixkareya were she-witches.

Coyote grinned, and thought some more, then trotted off to find an alder tree.

From the trunk of the alder tree Coyote pulled two large pieces of bark. Now, alder bark on the inside is very red, and so when Coyote had cut them into the shapes of fish, they looked a little like salmon. Seen from afar, they looked very much like salmon. Coyote smeared them with deer marrow, wrapped them in leaves, put them in his quiver, and set out for the witches' house.

Now, the witches were young and good looking, but did not have many visitors. So when, as they sat by their cookfire roasting acorns, they saw Coyote coming up the trail, they were pleased.

"He is very handsome," said the elder.

"Such a bright, shiny coat and bushy tail," whispered the younger.

"A fine evening, Ixkareya," called Coyote as he drew near.

"A fine evening," said the witches, nodding.

And so they talked together of the weather, then gossiped about the animal people of the foothills and the plain. As they talked, Coyote took a sideways look at the pond at the foot of the waterfall. There was no sign of salmon.

"Have some of our acorns, Ki-yoo," offered the elder witch as Coyote seemed about to go.

The younger held out the basket.

Coyote took a pawful and thanked them politely. "They will go well with my supper of fish," said he. He pulled one elder-bark salmon a little way out of his quiver so that they might see, and then pushed it back out of sight.

The two witches looked at each other as Coyote turned to go.

"Where did he get salmon?" hissed one.

"*No* one has salmon," muttered the other. "We should know."

They watched Coyote go, gathering wood on his way. He did not go far. On a flat place a little uphill from the house by the waterfall, he built a fire.

When it had burned down to a bed of bright coals, he speared his bark fish on a willow stick.

The two witches watched and whispered and frowned at each other as Coyote pretended to roast the fish over the fire. The deer marrow melted and spit as it spattered in the fire. The witches ate acorns as they watched, and wondered whether Coyote would offer them a share of the salmon.

He did not. And their mouths began to water.

"Since he has salmon, let us fetch some of our own," they said at last. And taking woven mats to hold over their heads, they stepped through the waterfall and vanished.

In a flash Coyote sprang up and dashed to the waterfall's side. He poked his head in through the water just far enough to see what lay beyond.

Beyond the curtain of water lay a great cave, and the great cave was filled with a pond greater than that which lay out under the sky. Behind the dam that made the great pond, the water flashed with thousands of salmon. There were so many salmon that the witches, standing at the pond's rim, had only to dip in their hands to pull out a fat fish.

"Tso!" crowed Coyote to himself. And he hurried back to his campfire.

At nightfall Coyote made a great show of yawning. He smoothed a place on the ground near his fire and made a bed of pine needles. Then he lay down and pretended to sleep. It was not easy, for he could smell the real salmon roasting.

At last, when the witches had eaten, one yawned and said, "I am sleepy, too."

"We must be careful," warned the other. "We must keep watch until the stranger has fallen to the bottom of sleep."

Coyote breathed deeply and sleepily, and all the while he listened. And all the while he listened, the witches argued whether he was truly asleep. So Coyote began to snore.

"Hai! I told you he was asleep," said the one, and together they went into their house.

When the moon went down behind the hill, Coyote slipped down across the trail and under the waterfall. There he set to work. He pried out rocks and pawed at the earth until he had made a great hole at the end of the dam. The water ran out in a rush, and with it the fish. Salmon swam past Coyote's legs and leaped over his back in their eagerness to be gone.

Inside the house of the Ixkareya, one murmured in her sleep, "Do you hear the waterfall laughing?"

But the laughter was Coyote's.

And ours. For if Coyote had not freed the salmon, there would be none in the Klamath River or the sea today.

8

Coyote Rides a Star

The animal people celebrated the return of the salmon with a feast more splendid than any they had ever had before. Though often they thought Coyote a great nuisance, they had to admit that he knew how to use his wits. At the feast—after much arguing—they even gave him the place of honor next to Eagle, their chief.

Coyote was full of himself. "Who in the World is more clever than Coyote?" he thought as he made his way home from the feast by starlight. "Who else could have snatched the Sun? Or sniffed out the stolen salmon? With my brains, I should be chief, not Eagle. *I* should have the best seat at the feast, and be served first. I, Ki-yoo the Coyote, should be honored above all others!"

Coyote gave a proud toss of his head, and as he did so, he spied the stars glittering in the dark sky above. A shooting star streaked overhead.

"Hai! How beautiful!" Coyote exclaimed. And suddenly he knew what he wanted most in the world to do.

"I want to ride on a star," said he. "Even Mouse

and Measuring Worm, the least of the animal people, can walk around on the earth. I, Coyote, should have a better way of going. And I shall! I shall take a journey on a star."

So Coyote climbed to the top of the nearest hill, lifted his nose to the sky, and howled up at the Evening Star. "Hai, Bright Star!" he called. "Come down here to me. I am going to take a ride on your back."

But the Evening Star did not obey. It barely blinked as it moved along its sky path.

"Ho! Are you hard of hearing, old Star?" cried Coyote. "I am Coyote—the Great Coyote, Sun-Snatcher and Fish-Finder. I have saved my people from darkness and cold and hunger, and now I wish to see all the World. Come down here so that I may jump onto your back."

The Evening Star smiled, but kept on its way without a word. In a little while it was gone.

But Coyote was not one to give up so easily.

At sundown the next day Coyote climbed to the same hilltop and called as he had called before. "Hai, Bright Star! Come down here to me so that I may jump onto your back."

This time the Evening Star, seeing that Coyote was in earnest, answered in a thin silvery voice. "Be content with your four feet, Ki-yoo the Coyote," it called. "Your place is on the earth. You may be a Great One among the animal folk, but you could not stand the speed of the stars."

But Coyote would not be put off. Each day at nightfall he returned and howled and yowled, whined and whispered and blustered and begged until at last Evening Star grew tired of listening.

"Enough, enough!" it said one night in a voice more sharp than silvery. "Jump on before I change my mind."

Evening Star slid down the sky, barely slowing as it skimmed past the hilltop, and then soared upward once more. Coyote gave a great jump, catching hold with his front paws, and almost slid off. "Hai, yi, yi!" he cried, but the sound whirled away in the star-wind. Evening Star flew so fast that poor Coyote could not haul himself up to crouch upon its back. It took all of his strength just to hold on.

Evening Star flew up and up and up, and then north over lands of ice and snow. The sharp star-wind grew bitter cold. Coyote's paws grew cold, then stiff, then numb, until he could hold on no longer. Letting go, he fell, head over feet over tail, back to earth.

He was a long time falling. Ten snows passed, some say. And when he came at last to earth, his

landing was so hard that he was—say some—
flattened out as thin as an acorn cake. Certainly,
from that day to this he has been thin.

And every day to this day, he climbs at nightfall
to the top of the nearest hill and scolds the Evening
Star.

9

Gopher's Revenge

Young Gopher and his little sister Cottontail were orphans. They had no father to teach them where to find the tenderest grass and sweetest roots, and no mother to teach them how to dig a dry, snug burrow. But they lived with their Grandmother Brush Rabbit, who was old and wise and had the answers to many questions. And so they learned these things, and many more.

But the first question little Gopher asked was, "Where is my father, Grandmother?"

And Cottontail, his sister, asked, "Where is my mother, Grandmother?"

"Ask me again when you are grown," said their grandmother with a shake of her head and a sigh.

So when summer's green leaves turned yellow in autumn, little Gopher asked once again, "Where is my father, Grandmother?"

And Cottontail, his sister, asked again, "Where is my mother, Grandmother?"

And once again their Grandmother Brush Rabbit shook her head and sighed. "Ask me again when you are grown."

So it went as each season passed, and always their grandmother gave the same answer. "Ask me again when you are grown."

When a year had passed and at last they were grown, Gopher asked once more, "Oh, Grandmother, where is my father?"

And Cottontail asked as before, "Oh, Grandmother, where is my mother?"

"Your father was killed when you were kits," said the old Brush Rabbit, "And your mother with him."

Gopher sat up straight. "Who killed them?" asked he.

Grandmother Brush Rabbit shivered. "The great Hagfish who lives in the river that flows by the hill," said she. "The Hagfish stung them dead with her dreadful sting. And of all the folk who went to find them, none came back again."

Gopher said nothing, but when he went out to dig roots, he went instead to a secret place he knew. There, a hole in the hillside led to a tunnel that led to the place where the river ran by the hill. At the tunnel's end he looked down and spied, sleeping in the shallow water in the shadows, the horrible Hagfish. Her eyes bulged out, her scales were hairy, and her teeth were shiny and sharp. The sting in her tail was long like a whip. Gopher looked and

looked, and then turned home again.

"Teach me to make arrows, my Grandmother," said he.

"I will," said Grandmother Brush Rabbit, but her heart was heavy. She knew what he hoped to do, and feared he too would never come home.

She showed him how to use an arrow flaker to shape arrowheads from stone, and how best to feather a shaft. Six times Gopher chipped away flakes from obsidian until what was left was an arrowhead. Then he trimmed and feathered six shafts. And when he had finished and gone, old Grandmother Brush Rabbit watched the river path and worried.

But Gopher left the path and went by the tunnel as he had done before. At the far end he looked out from the hole in the hill to spy the horrible Hagfish below. Then he put an arrow to his bowstring and shot. He shot again. And again and again until all of his arrows were gone, stuck in the ugly Hagfish. She roared and wriggled, tossed and thrashed, and lashed the stones in the stream with her terrible sting. At last she died. And when Gopher went down to the river's rim he saw a sight both sad and grim, for the stream was as full of bones as of stones.

At home, his sister Cottontail and Grandmother

Brush Rabbit were weeping by the cookfire when Gopher appeared.

"Gopher!" they cried, and ran to meet him.

"Grandmother," said Gopher. "I have been to the river that runs by the hill, and killed the old Hagfish who lived there." And he told of the river as full of bones as of stones.

The news went out that the terrible Hagfish was dead, and when the animal people heard, they came from near and far to give Gopher gifts. They brought shells and beads and feathers and seeds, and everything good to eat. And everyone danced and was glad.

And everyone still is glad, for it is thanks to Gopher that there is no Hagfish in the World today.

10

Clever Frog

One day Coyote went out hunting and had good luck. In the morning he shot a squirrel. At midday he caught only a mouse. But in the afternoon he shot a fine plump rabbit for his dinner. He had been hungry for days, and so, as he trotted home through the woods with the rabbit slung on his back, Coyote was pleased with himself.

Suddenly, where the path led out from under the trees and into the tall grass he spied a frog hopping along ahead of him.

"Ho!" cried Coyote, and he pounced, pinning poor Frog to the ground.

"What luck!" said Coyote. "Here is a nice juicy morsel to do me until I reach home and roast my dinner."

But as Coyote's teeth came close, Frog cried out in a great bullfrog voice. "Hold, Brother Coyote!"

Coyote stared at the little green fellow under his foot. "Why should I?" said he.

"Hai!" Frog thought quickly. "I meant to say, 'Don't eat me today.' For then you would miss tomorrow's race."

"Race?" Coyote's ears pricked up, for he loved

races. "What race? I have heard of no race."

"That is because I did not think of it before," said Frog. "You and I shall run a race, Brother Coyote, and if you win, you shall eat me on the spot."

"Agreed!" said Coyote, who could never turn down a dare or pass up a bet. For of course he would win, and Frog would taste as good—or better —tomorrow.

When it was agreed where and when they should meet, Coyote went on his way. Frog hopped down to the stream in the meadow to find his friends.

"I must run a race with Coyote tomorrow," said he to his friends. "At noon we will run from the spring to the alder tree at the bottom of the meadow and back. And if Coyote wins, he will eat me."

The other frogs threw up their hands and laughed at his foolishness. "Hai, Coyote will win! How can he lose?"

Frog grinned a wide grin. "He will not win if I have the help of my friends," said he. "Not if one of you goes early to hide by the alder tree. Not if when the others signal that Coyote is coming through the tall grass you give three jumps to make him think that I have been ahead of him from the start. I will hide near the spring, and when I see him coming I will jump over the finish line just before him."

Frog's friends agreed.

Late the next morning when Coyote arrived at the spring, Frog was there before him, hopping up and down as if he were eager to race. When the noonday sun was overhead, they started. Coyote dashed off as fast as he could go. Frog made three hops into the deep grass and sat down to wait.

Coyote raced on, but seeing no Frog at his heels or ahead, was sure he had left him far behind. Then, as he spied the alder tree before him, to his great surprise he saw the frog making his first hop into the turn around the tree.

"Now this is very strange," thought Coyote, and he ran faster still. "I did not see him pass me." On the frog's third hop Coyote shot past and called over his shoulder, "Fast, but not fast enough! I will wait for you at the finish line."

Coyote ran as fast as ever he had, but when he came in sight of the finish line there was Frog, making his last three hops.

"Fast, but not fast enough," said Frog as Coyote came panting up.

Coyote went home in disgust.

11

The Lost Brother

Back in the Beforetime, when young Weasel lived with his brother Mink, each morning Mink went out to hunt in the forest nearby. And each morning as he went, he told Little Brother Weasel to hide in the rafters of the house. "You will be safe there," said he. And Weasel obeyed.

But then one day someone came into the house singing, "*Tsa-tsa, tsa-tsa.*" The song was so sweet that Little Brother Weasel looked down from his perch and saw a tiny green lizard.

"Pretty, pretty," said Little Weasel, and he climbed down to play with the tiny lizard. After a while he gave him pele seeds to eat, and crisp fat from the meat his brother had roasted for the morning meal.

And as Lizard ate, he grew. The more he ate, the more he grew. Soon he was bigger than Weasel. Then bigger and bigger still. Little Weasel was frightened, and he began to cry. But before he could cry out, "Brother Mink, help me!" Lizard had picked him up, put him in his quiver, and carried him off.

When Mink came home, dragging the deer he

had shot, he called out, "Brother, are you here?" He looked for Weasel in the rafters, but he was not there.

"Where are you hiding, Little Brother?" he called.

No answer came, and Mink began to fear that Weasel had been stolen. He looked everywhere indoors and out, from the mountains to the sea. He asked all he passed where Weasel was. No one, neither the animal people, nor the trees, nor the rocks had seen him. Mink sat down at the sea's edge and wept.

The next morning the Mouse Brothers came to Mink's house to ask for a bit of meat. "Take as much as you wish," said Mink, weeping still. "I cannot eat it all alone."

The Mouse Brothers threw dust on their heads and wept loudly to show that they shared Mink's grief for Little Weasel. "Hai, it is sad to lose a brother. We know," said they, for they had lost more than one to hungry hunters.

While the Mice nibbled at his deer meat, Mink sat and thought. At last he said, "My brother was stolen by someone out gathering firewood. I am sure of it, for I found a bundle of sticks dropped outside my door."

"Then the thief cannot live far away," said the Mice. "For who seeks firewood far from his fire circle? You are sure to find your brother soon."

"Will you help?" asked Mink. "I must go to my older brother Bluejay, who lives to the south, to tell him the news. Will you go to ask Sun where Weasel is? Sun can see everywhere, from one edge of the sky to the other. I will give you feathers and beads and clay pots of paint if you will go."

The Mouse Brothers agreed. "We will go, and gladly."

First they took a long cord and tied it to an arrow. The arrow they shot straight up at the sky, where it struck firmly and stuck fast. The cord dangled down to the ground.

Mink came out of his house with the feathers and beads and paint. "Here are your gifts, and gifts for the Sun," said he, and he filled up their carrying sacks. "When you see Sun, do not be dismayed if he does not answer. You must run ahead on the sky-road and ask him again."

"We will," said the Mice, and they set off on their way. They climbed up the cord to the sky and sat down to wait at the side of the road Sun traveled every day.

At noon Sun came rolling along, carrying his daughter, Day Star, in a basket slung over his back.

"Stop, Sun!" the Mouse Brothers cried. "We have come from the Land Below to see you. We bring fine presents from Mink. Weasel his brother has been stolen away, and he has sent us to ask if you have seen him."

Sun rolled past, making no answer.

The Mouse Brothers remembered Mink's warning and ran on ahead. They stood in the middle of the sky-road and waited until Sun drew near again.

"Stop, Sun!" they cried.

Sun stopped. "I have looked," said he. "I did not see Weasel. But far to the east lives Lizard. Lizard has no children. Yet as I passed over his house this morning, I heard a child cry. Perhaps he has stolen Weasel."

"Yes!" cried the Mouse Brothers. "Surely the thief is Lizard."

So they gave Sun his gifts and shinnied down the cord to Mink's house as fast as they could go.

Mink had returned home without finding his older brother Bluejay, and his heart sang at the Mouse Brothers' news. He sent them on their way home with many thanks and as much deer meat as they could carry. Then he sharpened his arrow points with his flaker and rubbed his arrow shafts with Silver Pine pitch to make them strong. When they were laid out to dry, he curled up to sleep.

Early the next morning Mink strung his bow, filled his quiver with arrows, and set out toward the east. He traveled far and fast. At last he drew near to Lizard's country, a bare and stony land, and saw from far off Lizard's house. With magic, Mink made trees grow up to hide him as he crept closer, and closer still.

Now, Lizard had gone out that morning to catch ducklings in the tule grass at the edge of the lake to the west. "Stay in the house, my son," said he to Little Brother Weasel, "and guard my magic bow and arrows."

But Weasel knew that Lizard was not his father, and he turned away. When Lizard had gone and the house grew cold, Weasel did not stay in the house, but went out to look for firewood.

And there, behind a tree, he spied his brother Mink.

The two brothers danced with happiness, and then made haste to escape. But first, to punish Lizard, young Weasel took up firewood and ran into the house. When he had built a great fire, he broke Lizard's bow and arrows and threw them on the flames. Then Mink took out his arrow flaker, which had strong magic, and with it he and Weasel snapped themselves over the hills toward home.

Lizard was far away, but when he looked back toward his house he saw black smoke. Smoke, rising above the hill his house stood behind! He scurried home, and found his bow burned to ashes, and with it all of his arrows but two. These two he snatched up, and with the help of his own magic arrow flaker raced after the brothers.

Mink and Weasel snapped themselves from one hilltop to the next, but each time the speedy Lizard got ahead of them.

"Stop and fight!" shrilled Lizard when he had thrown his two arrows and missed. "Or give me back my new son!"

But Mink and Weasel kept on until, after many miles, Mink saw they must stop. Lizard's magic was as strong as theirs. They could not escape.

"Weasel is my brother and not your son," said Mink. And he put Little Brother Weasel in his quiver, out of harm's way. "I shall fight."

Mink fought, and bravely but, of the two, Lizard was the faster and stronger. Soon Mink began to tire.

Little Brother Weasel popped his head out of the quiver. "Oh, Brother, be careful! Look out!" cried he. "Hai! He almost hit you that time."

Mink and Lizard fought on, and Mink grew still more weary.

"Ai, if only our older brother Bluejay were here!" cried he. "Look out, Little Weasel, and tell me—do you see our brother Bluejay?"

"No," squeaked Weasel. "I see only the rocks and the sky."

Mink fought a little longer, then cried, "Look again!"

"No," piped Weasel. "I see only the trees rustling in the breeze."

"Look again," panted Mink, but he feared all was lost.

"No," wailed Weasel. "I see only a deer, coming this way."

But the deer was no deer, but Bluejay, out hunting deer with a pair of antlers tied on for a disguise. Looking up from the trail he followed, he saw the fight and recognized his brothers. He saw Mink stumble and fall to the ground.

At once Bluejay lifted his bow and shot wicked Lizard in the middle.

And the three brothers embraced and went happily home.

12

The War between Beasts and Birds

Once, back in the Beforetime, the animal people were divided by a quarrel, and the beasts and birds fought a great war. The beasts won the first battle, beating the birds back and killing many. Bat, as soon as he saw that the battle was going badly for the bird-warriors, dropped to the ground and crawled into a hollow log. There he lay hidden until the fighting was finished.

The beasts, proud of their victory, set out together for home, and as they passed his log, Bat fell into step beside them. The beasts were so full of boasting and songs that they went a long way before Raccoon saw Bat. "Hai! What is this?" he wondered aloud. "Why does Bat walk with us when he fought as a warrior against us?"

Bat, hearing this, protested. "Who me? I am no bird! Surely you can see that I am one of you and not one of the bird people? I have fur and fine, sharp teeth, like you, not feathers and a beak. Come, dear Raccoon, you are joking. What bird could have fur and teeth? Of course I am a beast!"

The beasts saw the sense of this, and let Bat walk along with them.

Not many days after the first fight there was another, which was won by the birds. As the beasts were being driven from the field of battle, Bat crawled under a fallen tree and waited. When the birds gathered to fly home, he slipped into the flock and took wing among them.

Halfway home, Sparrow Hawk spied him. "Hai! Hai! An enemy!" he cried.

"What are you doing here?" demanded the others of Bat. "You fought against us in the battle. Go back to your friends, the animals."

"The animals!" squeaked Bat. "No, they are our enemies. How can you think I am one of them? Do beasts fly? Have you ever seen one with wings?"

The birds had not, so they held their peace.

As long as the war lasted, Bat slipped back and forth between the beasts and birds, choosing always the winning side. Yet even so, he lost. For at the war's end the beast people and bird people held a council to decide what should be done about him. It did not take them long to decide. Eagle spoke for all when he said to Bat, "From this day you will fly only at night, and always alone. For from this day you have no friends, either feathered or furred, fliers or walkers."

· · ·

And from that day until this, it has been so.

13

Cricket and Mountain Lion

Cricket was proud of his house. It was small and round and snug, and sat in a shady spot safely away from the deer trail. Cricket had built it himself of mud and dung and fine grass, then rolled it into place beside a rotten log, and settled in.

One day Mountain Lion, out hunting, came stepping softly down the deer trail. Not far from Cricket's house his nose told him that a rabbit had crossed the path a moment before, and so he turned aside. As he padded past the rotten log, Mountain Lion heard a tiny shout.

"Hai, friend Lion! Stop where you are and step aside! That is my house. One step more and your paw will crush it."

Mountain Lion looked around to see who had spoken. When he spied little Cricket atop the log, he laughed. And then he roared until the leaves on the trees trembled.

"Miserable little creature!" he screamed. "Do *you* mean to tell *me* where I may walk? I am Mountain Lion. Not even Eagle can command me. Because I am strong and smart and swift, the forest is mine. And yet you dare to tell me where to step!"

"You may rule the forest, Big Paws," piped Cricket, "but I am Chief in my house and ruler of the land it sits on. So step aside. I do not care to have my house flattened."

Mountain Lion was amazed at Cricket's daring. "Indeed!" roared he. "I will flatten it and you too, if I wish. If I wish, little squeaker, I can crush you and all your folk under my paw."

Cricket gave an angry hop. "Hai, you think so? Take care. I may be small but I have a cousin not half so big as I am who is a great fighter. He can master a Grizzly Bear. So take care!"

"Ho-ho!" Mountain Lion laughed. "I must meet this brave warrior, little boaster. Bring your cousin to this place tomorrow, Cricket, and we will fight. He shall not master *me*. I will flatten him and you and your house together."

And he turned back the way he had come.

The next day at noon Mountain Lion came loping down the deer track and turned aside at the rotten log.

"Hai, small boaster!" he cried. "I am here. Where is your fierce little cousin?"

Cricket did not answer.

"Ho!" roared Mountain Lion. "Come out, brave cousin, and be crushed!"

Soon there came a buzzing by his ear, loud and

then louder still. And then a sharp, stabbing sting.

"Oh-ho-yo!" roared Mountain Lion. "Get out of my ear!"

But Mosquito, Cricket's cousin, only sang a louder song and went on stinging.

"Ai-hai-yi!" yowled Mountain Lion.

Cricket sat on his log and watched as Mountain Lion shook his head and leaped and howled. When at last poor Mountain Lion threw himself upon the ground and groaned, Cricket spoke up.

"Tell me, friend Lion. Do you mean to leave me and my house alone?"

"I will, I will, dear Cricket," moaned Mountain Lion. "Only call your cousin out of my ear."

So Cricket called Mosquito, and they sat together on the log and laughed to see Mountain Lion run away as fast as he could go.

He never ever came back.

14

Coyote's Squirrel Hunt

In the grassy ground under the oak trees at the edge of the plain were many holes. There squirrels lived, and there were many of them. Badger's house was not far away. Early every morning he took up a heavy stick and went there, and lay down upon the ground, each day in a new spot.

When the smallest squirrels came out of their holes Badger did not move. Not a twitch. So the little squirrels grew brave and drew close.

"He sleeps," whispered one.

"He is dead," said another.

They came closer.

"Asleep!"

"Dead!"

The little squirrels tiptoed closer still. They peered at Badger's paws. They pulled at his eyelids to peek into his eyes. They sniffed at his nose and squeaked to see his sharp teeth. They admired the streak of white on his head and nose.

"Nice," said some.

"Pretty," said others. And together they turned him over to admire his fur coat. They pinched and patted and climbed on his back, but Badger never moved.

"Dead," said the little squirrels, and went off to look for acorns.

Soon the half-grown squirrels came out of their holes and discovered Badger. And the same thing happened. They too looked and sniffed and pinched and went away. Last of all came the biggest squirrels. They too began to poke and prod, and debated how Badger had died. But no sooner had a number of good, fat squirrels gathered around, than Badger leaped up and killed them all with his club.

Every morning he picked another spot and did the same.

One morning Coyote passed by on his way to go fishing, and saw Badger lying like dead.

"No arrow," thought Coyote. "He has not been shot. What can be wrong?"

He hid in the shadows to watch, and soon a big squirrel stuck his head out of his hole. He was followed by others.

Coyote forgot about Badger. He thought of roast squirrel and wished he had his bow and arrows. There was nothing he liked better, he decided, than squirrel! Then suddenly, as quick as Coyote could blink, Badger bounced up and hit out with his stick.

One-two-three-four-five!

"Five! How did you do that?" cried Coyote as he trotted up. "Ah-hai! The stick! It is a magic stick."

"No," said Badger.

"Then what did you do?"

"Nothing," said Badger.

Coyote did not believe him. "Come, what did you do?" he asked, and once more Badger said, "Nothing." Coyote helped to carry the squirrels to Badger's house and on the way he asked again and again until at last Badger tired of his questions, and told him how to catch squirrels by doing nothing at all.

"Tso, tso!" Coyote laughed, for he loved tricks. "Tomorrow I shall go squirrel hunting."

That night, he could not sleep. He was so eager for morning to come that he kept getting up to see whether dawn had come. At the first light he took up a stout stick and set out to look for a good squirrel-hunting place. When at the edge of the forest he found one with many holes, he lay down and did not move.

The little squirrels came out first, just as Badger said. They peered into Coyote's eyes and pulled at his ears, and he thought of roast squirrel. They looked into his nose and played with his paws, and he could almost smell the squirrel soup. But then they rolled him over and climbed on his chest. Their tiny feet danced on his ribs.

And Coyote was ticklish.

He held his breath, but that was no help.

He tried to think of roast squirrel.

Of squirrel stew.

Of squirrel soup.

But nothing helped. Coyote began to laugh, and the little squirrels jumped up in the air in fright and dashed away.

So Coyote ate acorns for dinner.

15

Coyote and Badger

Coyote hunted all day and caught only a mouse and a lizard. His hunger grew bitter and sharp. So he thought to himself, "Badger, my brother-in-law, is more than a good squirrel hunter. He is a famous hunter of deer, and deer meat is almost as good as squirrel meat. Indeed, better, now I think of it. And though I cannot use Badger's squirrel-hunting trick, I *can* shoot deer. I will go out tomorrow with Badger to learn where he finds them. Then I will be the greatest of all hunters of deer!"

So it was that he rose before dawn the next morning and went to Badger's house.

"Dear Brother-in-law," said Coyote, "let us go hunting the deer together today."

"No," said Badger, for he liked best to hunt alone.

But Coyote teased and bothered and badgered him until at last Badger agreed. Together they traveled to the mountains and crept up through the chinquapin bushes toward the forest where many deer lived.

"Now," said Badger to Coyote, "we must separate. I shall go along the edge of the forest, and you must creep across the hillside down here. You will have first shot at every deer that comes up from the plain, and I will have first shot at any deer that comes down from the forest."

Coyote would have liked better to go along the edge of the forest, but he was impatient for the hunt to begin. Already he could almost taste the dark, juicy deer meat he would have to roast over his cookfire.

"Very well," said he, and he slipped off through the bushes. Now and again he raised up to see how Badger fared, and in the shadows under the forest's eaves could make out the white mark on Badger's head. But then the chinquapin bushes came to an end and Coyote could see only buckthorn ahead.

"Ow! Ho! Hai!" Coyote yelped as the thorns pricked at his ears and snagged in his coat. "Ho! Hai! Yow!" Surely, thought he, there must be an easier way to get deer meat.

But then Coyote looked up the mountain and spied a deer stepping down through the trees. "Hah!" thought he. "If Badger does not see it, it will come down past me."

He waited for a moment, then saw Badger put an arrow to his bow and raise it. Once, twice he shot. The deer turned and trotted on, and soon was out of sight. Coyote grinned. Badger, the great hunter, had missed!

Coyote raced up the hill.

"Brother-in-law," said he, as if he had not seen Badger shoot. "Did you see a fine deer come down through the forest a little while past?"

"I saw," said Badger. "I shot it."

"You shot it, Brother-in-law?" Coyote pretended to look around at the ground. "I see no deer. Come, you never shot at all."

"I did." Badger spoke calmly, for he knew Coyote's foolery well. "We will follow its tracks and see."

Together they followed the deer's tracks around the curve of the mountainside. They soon came upon the deer, lying dead with Badger's two arrows deep in its side.

"Tso! Two hits!" cried Coyote in admiration. He thought quickly. "Of course, had I been near enough to shoot, my arrows would be sticking in him too. Therefore, since we cannot both have the deer, we must settle which of us will take it home."

"Nonsense," Badger snorted. "It is mine."

Coyote paid no attention. He clapped his paws and cried, "A contest! We shall have a jumping contest. Let us stretch the deer out right here and mark the jumping line by his tail. He who jumps farthest shall have him." And before Badger could object, Coyote stretched out the deer, drew the jumping line, trotted back, took a long run up to the line, and jumped.

He landed by the deer's ears.

"Ai!" said Coyote to himself. "I can do better than that. But what does it matter? Little Brother-in-law Badger is so short-legged that I have won already. He will be lucky to jump as far as the short ribs."

Badger, knowing that to argue with Coyote was useless, walked back to take a long run. He barreled up to the jumping line and jumped clear beyond the deer's nose.

Coyote jumped up. "Loser tries again!" he cried quickly, and ran back across the jumping line.

The second time he jumped only as far as the deer's neck.

The third time he landed by the shoulders.

Again and again Coyote tried. Each try was worse than the last. When finally Coyote stopped and stood panting for breath, Badger began to drag his deer toward a level spot where he could more easily cut up the deer meat to carry it home.

"Ai, hai!" thought Coyote. "I must find some other way to beat him." Then he ran after Badger crying, "Stop, Brother-in-law!"

Badger turned and waited.

"The jumping contest was not fair. We must run a race," said Coyote as he caught up. "We will run a race, the winner will take the deer, and that will be the end of it."

"Hoh!" snorted Badger. "Off with you, Coyote! I won this deer fairly. He is mine and that is that."

Coyote planted his paw on Badger's back. "It was not fair, so we will run a race," said he. "Come, good Brother-in-law. If you beat me, the deer is yours."

Now Coyote was much bigger than Badger, and his foot was heavy on Badger's back. So Badger agreed to the race.

Coyote drew a new starting line. They made ready. They ran. And Coyote won, as Badger had known he would, for his legs were long and Badger's short.

"Tso!" exclaimed Coyote. "I win and the deer is mine. Lend me your knife and carrying sack."

Badger was already angry, and now he glowered and growled. "Why should I lend them? They are mine, and I will not!"

"How am I to get my meat home?" Coyote asked. "If I drag it all the way, my jaws will be too stiff for eating."

"That is no concern of mine," said Badger with a sniff. "If you were as clever as you think you are, you would find a vine to serve as a rope by which to drag your deer. I see one in a tree in the canyon below." And he pointed it out.

"Very well," said Coyote, but then he feared that as soon as he was gone, Badger would return and steal the deer. "There is no need for you to stay," said he. "I can manage by myself. Had you loaned me your knife and sack, we might have shared the meat, but now I will give you none. So trot off and shoot a deer for yourself."

"Gr-r-r," muttered Badger. But he turned and stumped off out of sight.

Coyote made his way down the canyon toward the tree where the vine climbed. He went a little way, then looked up to make sure that Badger had not returned. But he was nowhere to be seen.

Badger had not gone far. He stayed hidden until Coyote was far down the canyon, and then scurried back. With a *snick! slit! slash!* of his sharp stone knife he cut up the deer meat and stuffed it in his sack. Then he humped the sack on his back and started for home.

Coyote, once he had pulled a good length of vine from the tree, climbed back up the hill at a run. His brother-in-law, he knew, was a stubborn fellow, and he feared the deer would be gone. But the higher he climbed, the more broadly Coyote grinned, for there was no sign of Badger.

"Ha, hai!" Coyote crowed. "I was too clever for old Badger this time!"

But when he reached the flat place, the deer was gone.

"Tso!" yelped Coyote. "How dare that fat little fellow sneak back and steal my deer? I'll teach him to trick Coyote!"

He headed for Badger's house as fast as his long legs could take him. Soon he spied Badger himself far down the long canyon below.

"Hah, hai!" said Coyote in glee. "I have the thief now! I shall run along the mountain and cut down into the canyon ahead of him. When he comes by, I shall fill him with as many arrows as Porcupine has quills."

Coyote raced up and down along the mountain-side like a four-legged wind. When he reached the canyon floor, he crouched down behind a great boulder, taking care that his ears and tail were out of sight. His bow and arrow he held ready as he waited. And waited. And waited.

At last he raised his head above the boulder to peer up the canyon.

Badger was nowhere to be seen.

Nowhere, that is, until Coyote turned to look down-canyon. There, far off, was Badger with his sack on his back, heading for home.

"Hai, yowh!" Coyote howled, and stamped a foot in anger. "The fat little sneak has already gone by! He is faster by far than I thought. But next time I shall have him."

Coyote set off once more. He raced up the mountainside and up and down along the ridge above the canyon until he had gone far beyond the place he guessed Badger would be. In a flurry of stones and earth he plunged down into the canyon and hid behind an oak tree, his arrow ready against his bowstring. And waited. And waited. And waited.

"Hai, yai!" cried he at last. "Has the little thief passed me again?" And he ran a little way down-canyon until he saw, far off, Badger with his sack upon his back, heading for home.

Coyote was angry enough to eat Badger instead of deer meat. With a yelp and a yowl he scrambled back up the mountainside and tore along the ridge.

"I'll get him this time, the stumpy-legged cheat! Badger, you are as good as shot and skinned," he panted as he ran. "I'll eat you alive, I will!"

But down in the canyon once more, hiding behind a clump of willows, Coyote waited. And waited. And waited.

And once more, when he stuck his head out to look up-canyon, Badger was nowhere to be seen. Once more Coyote had not gone far enough. Once more, when he ran a little way down-canyon, there, far off, was Badger with his sack on his back, heading for home.

"Hai-yowh-oo-oo!" howled Coyote. He was angry enough to bite rocks. He ran straight down the canyon, not caring whether Badger heard him coming. His ears lay back and his long legs flashed. Far ahead, Badger's strong little legs scrambled faster still, but because he was so short, Coyote drew closer and closer.

He was only ten paces behind when Badger dived into his hole and was safely home.

After a little while Badger, in his house under the ground, heard a wheedling voice from above.

"Dear Brother-in-law Badger, truly I meant you no wrong. I should never have tried to trick you out of your deer. But I was hungry. I have not eaten in days," Coyote lied. "Will you not throw me a bit of the head?"

Badger only smiled to himself. He began cutting deer meat in strips to dry it.

"Ai, please!" Coyote pleaded. "A bite or two of leg meat and I'll go away."

Badger paid no attention at all.

"Then toss up some of the guts, dear Badger," begged Coyote in a voice full of tears. "I never meant to cheat you, Brother."

But Badger knew better than to trust Coyote again.

And at sundown Coyote gave up with a sigh and went home to a supper of lizard soup.

16

Mole and the Sun

One day back in the Beforetime, Sun decided that it would be easier to roll along the ground than across the sky. So, soon after he rose, when he thought no one was watching, he dropped down from the sky.

But Mole, who had gone out hunting early, saw, and ran to catch Sun as he fell.

"Hai, help!" squeaked Mole, shutting his eyes against Sun's great brightness. "The Sun has fallen!"

"What?" said some.

"Who called?" asked others.

"Hai, hai! Help me!" cried Mole again. "Sun has fallen, and he is heavy!"

All of the animals ran to help, and soon they had shoved Sun back into the sky, where he has stayed ever since.

But Mole's eyes still squint against the light, and his front paws to this day are bent back from holding up the Sun.

17

The Pine-Nut Thieves

When everything went Coyote's way in the village on the plain, he was so puffed up with himself that no one could stand his bragging tales and boastful airs. They hid in their houses when they saw him coming. But when things did not go Coyote's way, he was sure that everyone laughed behind his back. Then he packed his carrying sack and trotted off to live for a time with his brother Wolf in the country between the desert and the mountains.

One morning Coyote and Wolf lay in the shade of a willow tree and debated whether they should go hunting for jackrabbits or antelope squirrels.

"Jackrabbits are too fast for so hot a day as this," said Coyote.

"Squirrel, then," agreed Wolf. "Stewed squirrel will make a tasty meal."

Coyote sat up suddenly and sniffed the air. "Hai, Brother! What is that fine smell I smell?"

Wolf sniffed too, but his nose was perhaps not so sharp as Coyote's, for he said, "I smell nothing."

Coyote stood and sniffed the air again. "Someone is cooking. It is something I have never smelled before. Surely whatever has such a fine aroma must be good to eat. I think I must follow my nose and learn what it is."

"Follow it, then," said Wolf. "I shall stay here and hunt squirrels."

The smell was faint—only the silken thread of a scent—but no animal was so curious as Coyote. He trotted and sniffed and sniffed and trotted, climbing into the mountains as the delicious smell drew him. After a time he came into a country where he had never been. A place of mountain meadows, of pines and pinyons, it was the land of the Mountain Bluebirds.

One Bluebird saw Coyote coming from far off, and flew swiftly home to her village. "A stranger is coming! A stranger is coming!" she cried. "Hide your food, for a stranger is coming!"

Other Bluebirds took up the cry. "Hide your food! A stranger is coming!" For the Bluebirds ate only pine nuts, which they gathered from the pinyon trees, and they had none to spare. They scooped up their pine nuts and packed them into the cracks of the long roof supports of their houses to hide them.

"But it is time for the midday meal," said an old Bluebird. "We cannot turn a hungry stranger away. What shall we feed him? We have nothing cooked but our fine pine-nut mush."

"And he is very big," sighed another, looking out the door.

"We must feed him pine-nut mush," said a third. "But for each beakful of mush in the pot we will add a gourd full of water."

And they did so. They welcomed Coyote, and he sat down with them in the chief's house to eat the hot, watery mush. To the Bluebirds it tasted pale and thin, but from Coyote's first sip, his eyes shone. Such a glorious taste! Never had he eaten a food so rich and smooth and delicate. He savored every swallow.

Clearly, thought Coyote, the mush-soup was made from nuts. But of what kind? As he sipped, he closed his eyes to slits and slid a look around the house. The storage baskets stood empty. No sacks hung on the wall. Yet here and there on the floor were bits of what might have been husks or shells.

After the meal Coyote thanked the Bluebirds and turned toward home. Once out of sight of the Bluebird village, he hurtled down the mountain at a run.

"Brother Wolf! Brother Wolf!" called Coyote as he came near to their camp. "I climbed up to the Bluebird country and tasted their wonderful nuts. They are the best of all foods! I could not spy where they hide them, so I need your help. I must taste them again or die!" cried he.

Wolf and his friends Wood Rat and Pack Rat, Mountain Sheep, Pinyon Mouse and Pocket Mouse, Woodpecker, Yellowhammer, the Crow Brothers, and Hawk, hearing how tasty the nuts were, were eager to help. They would go all together to the Bluebird country.

They started out at once, and arrived that night. The Bluebird people made them welcome, and all night they played together at the Hand Game, calling out "Knife!" or "Leaf!" or "Stone!" Just before dawn Coyote began very softly to chant, "*Upija, upija, upija.* Sleep, sleep, sleep." One by one, the Bluebirds fell asleep where they sat.

At once their visitors sprang up and began to search. The rats looked in the baskets in each house, and under the mats. Mountain Sheep climbed among the rocks outside to look for hiding places. Woodpecker, Yellowhammer, Hawk, and the Crow Brothers searched through the trees, but found no sacks or baskets hanging in the boughs. Coyote and Wolf sniffed everywhere, their noses to the ground. But it was Pinyon Mouse who found the nuts at last as he crawled along the roof supports.

"Hai!" he piped. "Up here!"

Coyote stepped over the sleeping Bluebirds and took up a large empty basket. He called up softly to Pinyon Mouse, "Drop them down to me."

But Mouse's arms were too short and his paws too small to pull or pry the pine nuts free.

"Let me try with my beak," said Yellowhammer, and soon he had picked out all the nuts. In each house they found more, and by sunup the basket was full. The happy thieves slipped out of the village and headed for home.

The Bluebird people awoke to find their pine nuts gone. "The strangers have stolen them!" they cried. "Stop them! Stop them!"

"But how?" wailed others. "They are far away by now."

"We will stop them with magic," said the chief of the Bluebirds. "We shall make an ice wall so wide and tall that they cannot pass." And the Bluebirds sang together, weaving with a magic song a wall of ice that rose up in front of the fleeing pine-nut thieves. The great wall grew from the ground to the sky, and spread north and south as far as the sharpest eye could see.

"What shall we do?" cried Wood Rat, for the wall was too long for the animals to run around, and too high for Woodpecker and the other birds to fly over.

"It is only ice," said Wolf. "See, the Sun begins to melt it."

"But the Bluebird people will surely catch us

before it has melted," squeaked Pocket Mouse. "There are many hundreds of them and only twelve of us."

"Tso!" scoffed Coyote. "This wall looks thin enough. I can knock it down myself." He trotted uphill, turned, and dashed down to throw his weight against it.

And fell flat upon the ground.

Mountain Sheep tried next. "My horns," said he, "are better for butting." So he too trotted up a little way, then ran downhill to butt the wall.

And bounced right off.

Most of the others tried too, but all were smaller than Mountain Sheep, and none could knock the wall down. One after the other they tried, while the Crow Brothers sat on a tree branch and watched.

"Come, my black-feathered brothers," called Wolf when Hawk too had failed. "You too must try."

Coyote laughed. "Foolish Wolf! What good can such little folk do?"

No sooner had Coyote spoken than the smallest of the crows flew from the branch and climbed swift as an arrow so high in the sky that the animals below saw only a small black speck. Then down he flew like a feathered knife. He struck the ice so sharply that in that place it shattered, and shivered into pieces.

"Hei, hai!" crowed Coyote. He leaped for the hole in the wall, but Wolf, his brother, shouldered him aside. The mice and rats and birds jumped through, and only after Mountain Sheep had passed did Wolf follow. Coyote came last, muttering. "*I* discovered the pine nuts," growled he. "I should lead the way home."

He was still grumbling when the Bluebirds came. They swooped down the mountain like a swift blue cloud. They attacked the larger animals first— Wolf and Coyote and Mountain Sheep—pulling out tufts of hair and beating at them until they fell. Pack Rat, dashing away with the pine nuts, panted under their weight, and soon passed them to Wood Rat, his brother. Moments later, the Bluebirds caught Pack Rat and mobbed him. Wood Rat raced on ahead. When he too grew tired, and heard the whirr of the Bluebirds' wings, he passed the basket of pine nuts on to Woodpecker.

Before long, no one was left but Hawk. Though Hawk was strong, the basket was heavy and the Bluebirds were swift in their anger. So he stopped to hide the nuts quickly, and then flew on as fast as his wings would beat. When the Bluebirds caught up with him they dragged him out of the sky. They beat upon him and pulled out his feathers, but found not a single pine nut.

"Ai, ai, ai!" they cried to each other. "The thieves have eaten our pine nuts! What shall we do?" And they flew back to their mountain country, grieving as they flew.

Wolf awoke first, and shook Coyote. "Come, Brother," said he. "We must learn whether our friends are safe."

"And our pine nuts," put in Coyote. For though he was sick and dizzy, he was still Coyote, and greedy.

Together Wolf and Coyote went to find their companions. They helped them up and urged them on. Last of all they came to Hawk, who told Wolf where the pine nuts were hidden. And so, though they came home with fur and feathers ruffled and torn, the animals were as happy as they were safe.

Wolf at once took charge of the basket of nuts. "Our pine nuts must be planted, not eaten," said he. "For then pinyon trees will grow, and we will have sweet pine nuts every year, as many as we wish."

The pine-nut thieves agreed that it was the best of plans.

Except for Coyote. Coyote could not believe his

ears. Not eat them? The pine nuts he, Coyote, had sniffed out?

Wolf showed his friends how to plant the pine nuts. He took a mouthful of nuts to moisten them, then blew them far out across the land. In every place a nut fell, a pinyon tree sprang up. But when Coyote's turn at planting came, he quickly chewed up his nuts and swallowed them. When he blew, he spat out only spit, and where his spit fell there grew not pinyons but juniper trees.

And so to this day, because he planted no pinyons, when Coyote wishes for pine nuts, he must settle for the bitter berries of the juniper tree.

18

Coyote Rides the Sun

One day at sunset, back in the Beforetime, Coyote lay in the doorway to his house, and felt sorry for himself. "It is not fair," said he aloud to the clouds and sky. "What animal is as clever as I? Who has helped his people as much as I? Who has done more great deeds? The animal people should make me their chief, but they do not. Some even hide in their houses when they see me coming. How am I to show them how great I am?"

Just then, Sun rolled out of sight on his way down through the hole at the west end of the sky. Coyote, seeing this, sat up. He grinned.

"Hai, I have it! I shall ride the Sun across the sky! Everyone in the world will see me, and I shall be famous indeed. "But—" He frowned. "Where can I climb up to Sun's road? Perhaps Prairie Falcon will know."

Early the next morning Coyote went to Prairie Falcon's house. "Friend Falcon," said he. "Tell me how to get to Sun's road from here."

"Oh, that is easy," Prairie Falcon replied. "It is only a short hop from the top of the Easternmost

Mountain. You cannot miss it from there." And he showed him the road.

Coyote set off at a trot. But at midmorning, just as he reached the foot of the Easternmost Mountain, Sun looked over the mountaintop, and soon was hurrying westward across the sky.

"Stop!" called Coyote as he turned back toward the plain. "Stop, Sun, and hear me!"

But Sun rolled on without a word.

Coyote followed, shouting up to the Sun, but he got no answer. At last, as the afternoon shadows grew long, he found himself back where he started. Tired as he was, he went straight to Prairie Falcon's house, and told him what had happened.

"I am not so swift as you, friend Falcon," said Coyote. "When must I leave my house to reach the mountaintop on time?"

"Oh, that is easy," Prairie Falcon replied. "You must leave in the hour before dawn." And he showed him a shorter road to the mountain.

After his evening meal, Coyote went early to bed and sang to himself, *Awake in the hour before dawn, awake in the hour before dawn.* As he slipped into sleep, the song sang itself in his dream. *Awake in the hour before dawn.*

And he did. In the hour before dawn he took up his bow and his quiver of arrows and set out toward the east and the Easternmost Mountain. When he came to the mountaintop, he saw the Sun's road overhead. Looking out toward the eastern edge of the World, Coyote saw the Sun climb up into the sky.

"Hai!" said Coyote. "I will catch him this time." He crouched low to leap up onto the sky-road.

And landed in a heap on the ground.

"Hai! It is higher than it looks," said he to himself. "But I can reach it easily before Sun comes."

On his second try Coyote drew back a little distance and took a running jump . . . and again fell back to earth with a bump.

Coyote growled. "A short hop," Falcon had called it. But then Falcon had wings.

As the Sun drew nearer and nearer, Coyote gathered himself for one last leap. He hunkered down on his haunches and sprang up with all of his strength. But he fell, as before, back onto the mountaintop.

And Sun passed overhead, rolling away to the west.

"Stop!" howled Coyote as he scrambled down the mountainside. "Stop, Sun, and hear me!"

But Sun rolled on without a sign that he had heard.

Coyote followed, calling after him, but once more by late afternoon he found himself back where he started. If ever he was to catch the Sun, he saw, he must go all the way to the East Hole in the Sky at the eastern edge of the World. But how was he to find it? "I will ask Prairie Falcon," Coyote decided. "He will know."

And so, tired as he was, Coyote went to Prairie Falcon's house and told him all that had happened. "Friend Falcon," said he, "how can I find the East Hole in the Sky?"

"Oh, that is easy," Prairie Falcon replied, and he told him of the road on the far side of the mountains that led through the desert to that very place.

At dusk Coyote did not go hunting for his evening meal. Instead he went early to bed so that he could rise at middle-night for the journey to the hole in the sky. But he could not sleep. He saw himself astride the Sun, riding above the plains while all the animal people stared in wonder. He saw himself as chief, in Eagle's house. He saw Badger bringing him sacks of squirrels, Wolf coming with a pack full of pine nuts. He saw Bear come, bearing a big haunch of deer meat, and birds flocking to him with pele seeds and a fine feather cloak. The excitement was too much to bear. Coyote jumped up from his blankets, took up his bow and quiver of arrows, and raced off to the east by starlight. Better by far to be early than late!

Coyote ran all night, and came before dawn to

the hole in the sky at the eastern edge of the World. There he sat himself down at the very edge, his back to the hole, so that Sun could not come out. And he waited.

Before very long Sun came along. From below the earth he looked up and saw Coyote sitting there.

"Hai!" cried Sun. "Out of my way! Move out of my way so the day may dawn."

But Coyote did not move, and said not a word.

"Ho!" called the Sun. "Move away. I must not be late!"

But Coyote sat still, and made no sign that he had heard.

So the Sun shone fiercely up at Coyote, and Coyote grew hotter and hotter. He curled his tail up under him, but the tip stuck out and Sun singed it with his heat. Sun shone angrily on Coyote's back. As he grew hotter and hotter, Coyote spat on his paws and reached back to dampen down his coat.

"Hai!" exclaimed Sun at last. "*Why* do you sit in my way to make me late, Coyote?"

"I wish," said Coyote quickly—for he feared he would soon be roasted—"to ride you across the sky."

"Silly fellow!" said Sun. "No, never."

"Then I will not move," said Coyote. And he sat

tight, though he could smell the hair on his back and the tip of his tail as Sun singed it.

"I am late! I am late!" Sun fretted. And at last he agreed, and Coyote jumped upon his back. He closed his eyes against Sun's brightness, taking a look only now and again as Sun climbed up the trail to the sky. The first part was steep and had steps like a ladder, but as the trail grew easier, Sun hurried to make up the time he had lost. As he hurried, he grew hotter and hotter.

And so did Coyote.

"Ho, I am thirsty!" croaked he. "Give me a drink of water."

"Tso!" snorted the Sun, but he slowed and gave him an acorn-cup full.

Coyote grew hotter and still more hot. His coat began to smoke. He saw the clear blue of Clear Lake below and longed to jump down from the sky, but the Sun was too high. By midday the light was almost brighter than Coyote could bear, and he cried out to Sun to shine more gently.

"I cannot," declared Sun.

In a little while Coyote opened his eyes to see how far they had traveled, then shut them quickly again. A little later he took another quick look. And another. And this he kept up all afternoon to see how much closer they had come to earth. When at last Sun passed over the western mountains,

Coyote jumped into the branches of a tall redwood tree, and clambered down into the cool forest shade.

"Never again! No, never!" said he.

And that is why Coyote's back and the tip of his tail are dark, and why he does not come out at noonday, but hunts at dawn and dusk.

19

The Making of First Man

After his terrible journey with the Sun, Coyote for a long time lay around his house doing nothing. He did not hunt. He did not tend the fire. He did not cook. He left such work to his grandson Chicken Hawk. But Coyote was not one to lie still for long. After a while he grew restless and went out to look for something to do. But everywhere he wandered on the plain, all was well. Nothing needed doing. The animal people had sunshine by day and the moon at night, fire to warm them and to cook with, and salmon and pine nuts in season.

"I have succeeded too well." Coyote sighed as he returned home. "My people no longer need my help. But I must do something."

"You could gather wood for the fire," said Chicken Hawk when he heard his grandfather's lament.

But Coyote did not. He sat and watched Chicken Hawk stir the deer-meat stew, and at last an idea stirred in his mind.

"Hoh!" he said with glee. "I know what the World needs to set things buzzing. I shall make a new creature, and to show how clever I am, I shall make my creature more clever still. Who but Coyote could be so great-hearted as that?"

"What will you call him?" asked Chicken Hawk.

"I shall call him—Man!"

Coyote trotted down to the creek, where clay lay beneath the grass along the bank. He dug out a lump of clay and began to shape it. First he rolled a ball for the body, then a smaller one for the head. He rolled out four long legs and a tail. What else, thought he? It was not yet right. It was not right, but he did not know why.

"I will call a council," said Coyote at last. "And for a matter as great as this, it must be a council of all the animal people."

So he turned his nose up to the darkening sky and called. Then all across the plain, in voices rough and sweet and hoarse and shrill, the animals passed along his call. *Come to council! Council tomorrow! Come!*

And they did come. They came from far across the plain, and even from the mountains and seas and sands beyond. The fishes filled Coyote's creek, the birds bent low the boughs of the trees. The beasts came in twos and threes, and the bushes were heavy with crickets and spiders and bees. Mountain Lion and Grizzly were there, and Deer, Wolf, and Antelope. Turtle came, and Fox and Ferret and Mountain Sheep. Mice of all sorts and

Rats were there, and Beaver came, and Badger, and more. When the animals had seated themselves in a wide circle, Coyote sat down in its center and held up a paw for silence.

"I have decided to make a new creature I shall call Man to rule over us all," announced Coyote. "But to make him the best that I can, I need your advice. I know what his spirit should be, but what of his shape and strength?"

"Tso!" exclaimed Mountain Lion. "If Man is to rule Grizzly and me, you must give him a roar that will make the rocks on the mountain tremble. Give him long hair and broad paws with terrible talons for his claws. Then, hoh! All will rush to obey him." Mountain Lion laughed to see Mouse shiver and cover his eyes.

"Gr-rr-r!" grumbled Grizzly. "Give Man such a voice and he will have no one to rule, no game to hunt. Everyone will hide! No, give him a voice that can be loud or soft, and the sense to know when to roar and when to whisper. You must also give him swift, sure feet, and strong forelegs to grip his prey."

"Hunh!" snorted Deer. "You forgot that he will need antlers to fight with. He would look foolish without them. As for his voice, I agree with Grizzly. He will not need a roar to rattle rocks on the mountainside. Now, eyes and ears—they are a different matter. I say, let Man have ears that can hear a spider's footstep, and eyes that can see either a fox or a flea from afar. Then he will always know danger when it approaches."

"Antlers? Ah, bah!" bleated Mountain Sheep. "He would always be tangling his head in a bush or snagging himself on a tree limb. A horn rolled up on each side of the forehead—now that would be both handsome and practical. With horns Man will be able to butt much harder."

"Hai, yai!" exploded Coyote. "A fine help you are! You are all the same. No brains. Each of you has described himself. What is the use of that? Why not call your children 'Men' if that is all you wish? Now, I may think well of myself—"

Some in the crowd laughed aloud.

Coyote ignored the laughter. "I may be both clever and wise," said he, "but I wish Man to be just as wise and clever. Certainly he will have four legs, and five toes to each foot, but his feet should spread out straight, like Grizzly's. Then he can walk on either four legs or two."

Coyote paced back and forth across the circle of animals as he spoke. "As for Man's tail: though none is more handsome than mine, it would be better to be tailless, as Grizzly is. Of what use is a tail but for fleas to ride on? And I do not mind if Man has a voice like Mountain Lion's, so long as he is not always roaring. But why a long coat of hair? That would be too hot in summer. Why should he not be like Fish? Fish is cool in the hottest summer, and swims under ice in the winter. Man will be comfortable all the year if he has fish's skin."

Some of the animals frowned and others nodded as Coyote went on.

"Claws like Eagle's would be useful for carrying," he said. "But for running and digging, paws like mine will be best."

"Not so fast!" piped up Gray Lizard. "Man will need hands, not paws. Hands like mine can run as fast as paws, and hold, and pull, and make tools. No hands are better than mine. Paws, indeed!"

"He will have paws!" snapped Coyote. "Nothing is better for digging. When Squirrel goes down his hole, I can root him out in a moment."

Eagle shook his head. "Gray Lizard speaks wisely. With hands like his, Man's mate can make baskets and Man bows and arrows."

Gray Lizard laughed. "And they will be able to play shinny ball better than Coyote. See, Coyote, what my hands can do!" And he picked up a stick like a shinny-ball bat and swung it, then picked up a stone the size of a shinny ball and tossed it from hand to hand.

"Hands! Hands!" cried some in the crowd.

"We will take a count," said Grizzly. "How many wish Man to have hands? To have paws? Tso! Coyote, the council has spoken. Your Man must have hands like Lizard's."

"Very well," said Coyote, hiding his anger. "And Deer is right. Man should have eyes and ears as sharp as his. These, and Mountain Lion's voice, Grizzly's feet, Fish's skin, Lizard's hands. All these he should have, and brains like mine." Coyote looked around the great circle. "I thank you for your help. Now I shall go to work."

"Wait! Wait!" burst out Beaver. "This is still a council. The council must decide, not Coyote alone. You say Man is to have no tail. No tail, indeed! Never have I heard such foolishness. Everyone needs a broad, strong tail. How is this Man to move mud and build his lodge without one?"

"Hoo!" hooted Owl. "You may be clever, Coyote, but you are not wise. Four legs, indeed! Wings are what he will need. Wings!"

"Puh-puh-puh!" snuffled Mole. "What use are wings? If I had wings I would always be bumping the sky and falling. It is better to stay safe on the ground. And why give him eyes for the Sun to burn? Better to give him a silky fur coat and let him dig a fine burrow where he may sleep away the day."

"What nonsense!" piped Mouse. "Man will need

the sunshine to warm him when his nest grows cold toward morning. He will need eyes to find the seeds he eats."

Screech Owl ruffled his feathers. "Skre-e-eek!" he began, but before he could speak, Coyote covered his ears with his paws.

"Ai-ee-yowh!" he cried. "Enough! Go home! I will make Man my own way."

"I too. I will make Man myself, snarled Mountain Lion.

"And I!" growled Grizzly.

"And I!" squeaked Squirrel.

"And I!" chirped Chickadee.

"And I!" barked Fox.

"And I!" snapped Turtle.

"And I!" chorused the other animal people as Coyote turned and ran home to his house. Together they rushed, snapping and snarling, to the creek where the clay lay under the grassy bank. And each took away clay and began to shape a figure that would be Man.

Coyote labored all afternoon. When the others went off to hunt for their dinner, he worked on without stopping. Long after dark he worked, and then he went down to the creek to listen. On all sides he heard only snores. So he fetched a pitch-lined water basket, and crept back down to the creek to fill it. Then he slipped from one sleeping

animal to another, pouring water on each of the soft clay Men. When they all were washed away, he returned to his house and worked on.

At the very last, Coyote looked at Man's paws and decided that the council had been right after all, so he reshaped the clay to make hands like Gray Lizard's. Then, when the Morning Star rose and dawn was not far off, Coyote was finished. His clay Man lay on the grass in the starlight.

"Shine on him, Morning Star," called Coyote softly, and he touched Man's hand with his paw.

"Man, you were begun in the daytime," Coyote whispered. "Therefore you will like the sunshine best. You were finished in the nighttime, so you will not be afraid in the dark. Be cunning by light and by dark, and you will rule even Coyote."

Then Morning Star shone her beams full onto Man's face.

And Man opened his eyes.

20

The Waking of Men

Coyote was so pleased with First Man that he decided to make others of his kind with his magic. So he gathered feathers, and stuck them one by one in the earthen floor of his sweat-house. *Feathers,* he sang, *be Men. Be Men. Be Men.*

The next morning when he went to look, all of the feathers had turned into Men and Women, and all of the Men and Women were awake, for their eyes were open. But all day they lay still, and spoke not a word.

"Are they not handsome?" said Coyote to his grandson Chicken Hawk.

"Yes, Grandfather," said Chicken Hawk. "But they do not talk. Are they sick?"

"Hum," said Coyote, for he did not know. "I will ask Old Man Moon." For what Coyote did not have or did not know, Moon did.

Coyote took his carrying sack and traveled south to the nearest hill. Climbing to the top, he sat himself down and called, "Old Man Moon! Are you there?"

"I am here," said Moon.

"I need words," Coyote said.

"How many?" asked Moon.

Coyote held out his sack. "As many as you can spare."

"I do not need many myself," said Moon, so he poured in some words and tied up the neck of the sack. Coyote slung it on his back and hurried home. He emptied the sack out on the floor and at once the Men and Women began to talk.

"What a fine sweat-house this is," said one.

"The finest I have seen," said another.

"What a fine-looking animal Father Coyote is," said a third.

"And Chicken Hawk too," observed yet another.

Coyote listened as the people talked on into the darkness, then one by one fell silent and slept.

On the second morning young Chicken Hawk pulled at Coyote's ear to wake him. "Grandfather," said he, "in the sweat-house the people are talking, but they do not move. Are they sick?"

"Tso, tso," said Coyote. "That is not good." And so he went south to look for Old Man Moon. "Old Man Moon, are you there?" he called.

"Hoh!" said Moon. "I am here."

"Moon," said Coyote, "I need some fleas."

"Fleas! Very well," Moon said, and he gave Coyote a small black pouch. "But do not open the pouch before you reach home."

Coyote thanked Moon and trotted north toward home. But after a while he began to wonder, and he felt the black bag. "It feels empty to me," thought he. "Moon has given me the wrong bag."

So Coyote stopped and loosened the cord to take a look. At once five hundred fleas leaped out onto his nose, scurried into his fur, and began to bite. They bit him on his ears, his belly, his chin. They bit him here and there and everywhere, while Coyote yelped and rolled in the dust on the road.

"Enough, enough!" he cried. "Go back in the bag, go back in the bag!" When they did, he tied up the bag and went on, still itching and scratching.

But when in the early evening Coyote arrived at his sweat-house and shook the fleas out on the Men and Women, he decided it was worth all the itching. For his people began to twitch, then to scratch. One sat up and scratched his head. Another stood and scratched his side. A third hopped on one foot and scratched the other. Soon all of the people were moving, and they walked and talked together until night fell.

On the third morning, once again Chicken Hawk came to wake Coyote. "Grandfather," said he, "surely the people are sick. I have brought them mice and lizards and beetles, but they will not eat."

"Hei, hai," said Coyote. "I know what they need.

I must visit Old Man Moon again." And he took up his carrying sack and trotted off south as before. When he came to the hill, he climbed to the top.

"Well?" said Moon, who had seen him coming.

"Moon, my people need bread and pinole and mush," said Coyote.

"Very well," said Moon, and he filled up the sack with pinole and mush, and put a large piece of acorn bread on the top.

When Coyote reached home, he divided the food and gave each Man and Woman an equal share of the mush and pinole and bread. And after their meal they all went to sleep.

On the fourth morning Chicken Hawk awakened Coyote and said, "Grandfather, the people are sick. They walk and talk and eat, but they do not laugh."

"Tso, tso!" said Coyote. "I should have thought of that." And he went off to the south again to find Old Man Moon.

"Well? said Moon when he saw him coming. "What now?"

"I need some laughter," Coyote said.

"Very well," said Moon, and he gave Coyote a bright yellow bag. "But you must take care. Do not open the bag before you reach home."

"I will not," said Coyote, remembering the fleas.

But the bright yellow sack was so light that before he had gone far, Coyote began to wonder if it were empty. "Surely laughter is heavier than air," thought he. Then he remembered Moon's warning and went on. But when he was almost home he stopped again. "I must look!" said he, for his curiosity itched more than any fleabite. So he untied the bag and looked in.

At once Coyote felt a tickling everywhere, on his chin, his belly, his ribs, and he laughed. He fell down in the road and rolled over with laughter. He chuckled and giggled and snickered and roared. "Enough, enough!" he cried. "Go back in the bag! Go back in the bag!" And when it did, he tied up the bag and ran home, laughing all the way.

That night, while the new people slept, Coyote crept into the sweat-house and poured the sack of laughter over them all.

And when they awoke the next morning, they were real Men and Women at last.

21

The Last Council

The news of First Man's waking swept through the animal villages like wind across the grassy plain. Old Man Above, hearing the news, summoned Eagle and Coyote to the great white-teepee mountain, Mount Shasta. There he told them that with the coming of Man, the Beforetime was at its ending.

"And great will be the changes," warned Old Man Above. "For in the Aftertime to come, no longer will your folk be both animals and people, with the powers of both. No longer will any among you be shape-shifters and workers of magic. You will be animals only, and only Man will have the powers of speech and spirit. Coyote has made Man worthy to rule, so rule he will." Old Man Above rose. "You, Eagle, must call all of the animal people to a Last Council. The council will meet here, at the foot of my mountain at sunrise nine days from today. You, Coyote, must tell First Man to come, and tell him this also: that he must make as many bows and arrows as there are animals. These he shall bring with him, and the animal to whom he gives the longest bow shall have the most power among you. He to whom he gives the shortest shall be the least of all living creatures."

Eagle and Coyote went down from the mountain, Eagle in sadness for the Beforetime that was ending, and Coyote in secret glee, for at last he saw how he could be chief of all the animals. He raced home to tell First Man to make the bows and arrows.

For eight days First Man worked, making and stringing bows and feathering arrows. The animals, not wishing to be late to the Last Council, set out before Man for the white-teepee mountain in the north. Coyote traveled with them, and together they came to the council place at sunset.

The animals lay down together to sleep until sunrise and the coming of First Man, but Coyote was too cunning to sleep. Above all things he ever had wished for, he longed for the power over the other animals that the longest bow would give. With it he would be the greatest of hunters. He could hunt and eat whatever meat he wished—eat as *much* as he wished! But Coyote, for all his cunning, could think of only one way to make sure that he was the winner of the longest bow.

He must stay awake.

All night.

If he could stay awake, he would be the first in line at sunrise, and all would be well. First Man,

coming with his bows and arrows, would see his
Father Coyote waiting to greet him—Father
Coyote, who made him. To whom else could he
award the longest bow? Coyote chuckled to himself
as he lay down and rested his nose on his paw. How
jealous Mountain Lion and Grizzly and Eagle
would be!

After an hour or two, Coyote yawned. He sat up
in alarm and shook his head to clear away the sleep.
But when he lay down again, sleep crept closer still.
His eyelids drooped.

"Come, this will not do!" thought Coyote as he
struggled to his feet. He rubbed his eyes. Then he
trotted around the camp to clear his head, and soon
was wide awake. Yet when he lay down again, sleep
soon slipped over him. His eyelids closed.

"This will never do!" thought Coyote as he
dragged them open again. So he began to hop and
skip around the camp, and soon was wide awake
once more.

"Hoo-oo!" said Owl, who stirred and opened one
eye. "Who is that hopping?"

"Ee-eee!" squeaked Bat as he stirred and pricked
up an ear. "Who is that skipping?"

Coyote stopped still, and sang his magic song.
"*Upija, upija,* Sleep, sleep," he sang. "Sleep well,
sleep deep." Then he crept back to his place beside
the path Man would follow up from the plain, and

paced up and down, singing softly to himself, "*Wake, wake, awake!*" But by the time the Morning Star rose in the dark sky, Coyote could keep his eyes open no longer. He had tried holding them open with his paws, but his paws too grew heavy with sleep. So at last, from a bush close at hand he broke off two sharp little twigs to prop open his eyelids.

"Now I am safe!" thought Coyote. And he settled down to watch the Morning Star, resting his nose on his paws.

Morning Star climbed quickly up the sky. At first light of dawn Lark and Meadowlark began to sing. Bear and Mountain Lion rumbled and grumbled and stretched their legs. Squirrel and Spotted Skunk stirred. But Coyote slept on, for the sharp little twigs had slipped and pinned his eyes shut. The Sun rose, the animals went to meet Man, and still Coyote slept.

Man came striding up from the plain with the great bundle of bows on his back and in each hand a sack of arrows. He untied the bundle, spread the bows out on the ground, and chose the longest. Then he stood straight and looked around at the crowd of animals gathered there at the mountain's foot. And he pointed the bow.

Mountain Lion came forward to take the longest .

bow, and with it he took the greatest power among all the animals.

Man gave the next-longest bow to Bear, and those next to that in size to Eagle and Wolf. Others he gave to others, as he judged they deserved, until only two remained. When he had given a bow to Frog, only the smallest of all was left.

"Whom have I missed?" called Man. "Come forward, Little One, and take your bow."

But no one stepped up to claim it. Man called a second time and a third, then told the animals to search their camp and down along the path beyond. This they did, and so at last came upon Coyote, fast asleep.

"Hai!" exclaimed Badger. "Why has the foolish fellow fastened his eyes shut?"

"Hoh!" laughed Fox. "Clever Coyote has out-foxed himself again!"

The other animals crowded close, and looked and laughed. Jackrabbit jumped on Coyote and danced upon his ribs, and everyone Coyote had tricked or chased joined in in turn. When they could laugh no more, they lifted him up and carried him off to Man.

"Father Coyote!" cried First Man in surprise. "So it is you who are last!" With a shake of his head he pulled out the sharp little twigs and gave Coyote the last of the bows.

"Shoot! Shoot!" shouted the animals.

Coyote put a tiny arrow to the tiny bow and shot, but the arrow flew barely a foot. The animals laughed again, and Coyote hung his head.

Only Man did not laugh. It pained him to see Father Coyote the weakest of all, weaker even than Frog. Lifting up his arms to the white-teepee mountain, First Man called, "Old Man Above, is there nothing I may give Coyote to comfort him in his weakness?"

Old Man Above looked down. He saw Coyote standing before Man, his head down in shame, his tail between his legs. "Very well," said he. "I shall give Coyote great cunning, ten times greater than before."

And so it was that Coyote could lift his head in pride once more.

But to this day he runs with his tail between his legs.

22

Dog's Choice

At the end of the Last Council of the animal people, Eagle spoke to the beasts and birds. "Now," said he, "has come the time. No more are we 'the Animal People.' We must go from this place and live with folk of our own kind, falcon with falcon, deer with deer and bear with bear. No longer will we live together in houses in villages as when we were people, but each in the place that fits his nature, birds in their nests, wolves in their dens, and bears in their caves."

So it was that as Eagle named each kind and its dwelling, those beasts and birds went down from the foothills of the white-teepee mountain to seek out new homes in the wide World. At the last only Eagle and Coyote and his cousin, Dog, were left.

Coyote was suddenly afraid. In all his cunning and all his planning he had never thought that the animals would be driven apart by the coming of Man.

"Friend Eagle," said he, "I will come with you and hunt with you, and live on your mountaintop."

"You cannot," said Eagle. "You have no wings."

"I will ask Old Man Above to give me wings," said Coyote eagerly.

Eagle shook his head. "Then you would not be Coyote. No. Go instead with Dog, who loves company. He is your cousin, and will be your friend if you will have it so." Then, with a cry of "Farewell!" he beat his great wings and rose into the morning air.

Coyote sat for a moment feeling sorry for himself, but then a crafty look came into his eyes. "Tso, friend Dog! It is a beautiful day. What shall we do with it?"

Dog wagged his tail happily. "Whatever you wish. We can lie here and do nothing. That would be nice. Or we can run around to see what everyone else is doing. That would be interesting. Or we can go hunting and share what we kill. I like to hunt." He grinned.

"Very well," said Coyote. "Let us hunt, but I will be chief hunter. You must follow off to the side and chase the game over to me."

"Good! I shall like that," said Dog, and he trotted off into the trees, his tail wagging, and set to work.

First Coyote caught three squirrels, but when Dog came panting up for his share, Coyote had eaten all three.

"Where is my share?" asked Dog.

"I am sorry, dear Dog." Coyote shook his head sadly. "I did not mean to eat them all, but I ate not a bite yesterday, and was so hungry that I could not help myself. Believe me, the very next game I kill will be yours."

The next game that came to Coyote's sharp teeth was a fine, fat rabbit, but when Dog came trotting up, nothing of it was left but fur and bones and Coyote licking his lips.

"I was hungrier than I thought," said Coyote. He hung his head as if in shame. "I promise, the next shall be yours, good Dog."

But the next was not, nor the mice nor the gophers after that.

And Dog grew wise at last.

"I grow weak from hunger, cousin Coyote," said he. "And I see that to eat I must leave you and fend for myself."

Coyote was alarmed. "No! No, dear Dog! You would not like such a lonely life. From now on I will give you your share."

Dog did not believe him. "No, you will not. Without even hunting I can eat better than I do with you. I shall follow behind Men when they hunt, and eat from the bones they leave."

"Ai, no!" pleaded Coyote. "Only stay, and I shall chase the game to you, dear Dog."

But Dog would not stay. He went off down the trail and left Coyote behind. For many hours he ran, then trotted, then walked, and grew as weary as he was hungry. At last he saw the village on the plain where Men and Women now lived. Very slowly he drew near, for he feared that they would chase him away.

But the people saw him coming from afar and went out to meet him. They brought fresh meat. They laid their hands upon his head. And they said, "Welcome Dog."

So it was that Man and Dog walked together out of the Beforetime and now, in the Aftertime, walk together still.

Author's Note

The Indian tales of *Back in the Beforetime* come from a number of California tribes, from the Klamath River region in the north to the inland desert mountains and the southern coastlands. In reading through the many tales and fragments of tales recorded during the past century, I chose first those legends which could be woven together to tell the larger tale of Creation from the making of the world to man's rise to lordship over the animals, and then a selection of comic or trickster folktales which seemed to fit happily within that framework. In several instances, where a story was incomplete or lacking in detail which could be found in a second version from the same or another tribe, I have told a composite tale.

Several of the California tribes are represented in *Back in the Beforetime* by more than one tale, and many by none. Being a storyteller rather than a folklorist, I have not sought to make a representative collection, but one which will offer to readers or to a storyteller's audience entertaining tales that can both stand alone and give some sense of what the context of a single story might have been within a tribe's traditional body of tales.

Many Californian tribes have dwindled or vanished. Others still struggle to preserve their traditions and holy places in a world of change. Of some, little trace is left but their tales, recorded long ago by folklorists and anthropologists. For us their tales of the Animal People, in whom animal and human natures are mingled, are both comic and poignant, reminding us that once there was a time when Man was more fully at home in the natural world.